stoLeи тıме

by Vangelis Hatziyannidis

Translated from the Greek by Anne-Marie Stanton-Ife

Drawings by Nana Vetta

MARION BOYARS
LONDON • NEW YORK

Vangelis Hatziyannidis was born in 1967 in Serres and

Praise for *Four Walls* also by Vangelis Hatziyannidis and published by Marion Boyars:

'Vangelis Hatziyannidis' first novel delightfully blends the serious...themes of imprisonment and solitude with humour, humility, horribly violent deaths, coincidences and miracles – all of which add up to a witty fable, satisfyingly replete with the essential ingredients of magical realism.' *The Guardian*

'Probably the most atmospheric Greek novel of the year,' Greek *Vogue*

'Charming in its slow-motion evocation of Greek rural life and the peculiarities opened up by isolation... *Captain Corelli's Mandolin* goes gothic.' Kirkus Reviews

stoLen time

Published in Great Britain and the United States in 2007 by
MARION BOYARS PUBLISHERS LTD
24 Lacy Road, London SW15 1NL
www.marionboyars.co.uk

Distributed in Australia and New Zealand by
Peribo Pty Ltd, 58 Beaumont Road, Kuring-gai, NSW 2080

First published in Greece by To Rodakio as O PHILOXENOUMENOS in 2004.
Printed in 2007
10 9 8 7 6 5 4 3 2 1

Translated with the support of the Culture 2000 programme of the European
Union.

Education and Culture

Culture 2000

A CIP catalogue record for this book is available from the British Library.
A CIP catalog record for this book is available from the Library of Congress.

ISBN: 0-7145-3126-X
13 digit ISBN: 978-0-7145-3126-7

Set in Bembo 12pt
Printed in England by Cox & Wyman
Cover design by Holly Macdonald

'When I read the several dates of the tombs, of some that died yesterday, and some six hundred years ago, I consider that great day when we shall all of us be contemporaries, and make our appearance together.'

Joseph Addison, *Reflections in Westminster Abbey*

one

It was Filippos Argyriadis's opinion that counted. He was their leader although no-one understood how his influence over the other four had established itself and no-one acknowledged that it had. He hadn't volunteered; he hadn't been asked. It had just happened. He was their leader. Everyone paid attention when he spoke. Whenever there was a difference of opinion, the final view bore the stamp of his will. Whenever he disagreed with one of them, the others always took his part. Even the director, Petros Halkiolakis, who deep down resented him, always sided with Filippos Argyriadis.

Disagreements were, however, rare. Each of the four had developed another side, a second side that enabled them to get along with and fit in with the others in the group – with their second sides, that is. It was remarkable to see their faces change as soon as they got together, in the same way that the walls of a stage set rotate all at once to transport the audience from the drawing-room scene, let's say, to the morgue scene. Those second sides were like that. They had developed gradually, because in the beginning, when they were still very young, they argued constantly. But even then, the conflict was confined to two people, and did not erode the unity of the group. These collisions gradually petered out with the emergence of each member's second side, which consolidated their position in a five-link chain. If any of the five came under attack from an outsider, things would follow a set course: the group closed ranks round the member and the outsider soon came to realise that he was dealing not with one but five adversaries. But the opposite never occurred; if one of the five links fell under the spell of an external friendship or romance from the outside, the group had a hard time accepting it, and smiles in such cases were rare.

The only exception to this was Skouris. Skouris was the fifth link. His arrival served to unite the four permanent members. 'I'm getting married,' came the abrupt announcement from Ioanna Chryssovergis one day, and shortly thereafter she introduced them to Simos Skouris, a goldsmith. After a couple of years this new member had become fully absorbed into the historic nucleus. His temperament had helped; over the course of those two years he had developed an admirable second side, and was looked on as though he had always been around. That's how they became five. I picked all this up from conversations I had with Tina Paraschis, the photographer.

Halkiolakis and Argyriadis went back a long way; they were old school friends and it was while they were still at school that they met Ioanna Chryssovergis and Tina Paraschis at amateur dramatics. It was then that Halkiolakis got the idea that he wanted to go into directing, and Chryssovergis decided to become an actress. Paraschis took up photography.

I can't say for sure when it was that Filippos Argyriadis got involved with antiques and paintings. All I know is that his business card did not read *Dealer in Fine Arts* but *Collector*. Skouris, deliberately needling him, would say:

'You and I are colleagues of sorts. Both merchants. I sell gold, you sell antiques.' Argyriadis would answer: 'I am not a merchant.' 'What do you mean, you're not a merchant? You buy, sell, run a shop, all of which makes you a merchant.' But Argyriadis was adamant that he was essentially a collector, who bought and sold for the sole purpose of renewing his collection. Even his shop served the same general purpose. 'I only sell the pieces I'm tired of looking at. I use the money from their sale to acquire new pieces; that is how I maintain a collection, one which might not grow but certainly evolves.'

The actress was an admirer of Argyriadis. They all admired him, but in her case it was more obvious. The collector was not demonstrative by nature; nobody felt completely at ease with him and he came across as a cold man. It is possible that his kudos derived from this fact. The actress tried to laugh and joke with him all the time, thinking that was the way to get close to him. The others also reserved a special treatment for him – a form of respect. He enjoyed all this attention, taking it as a sign that he was entitled to special privileges. Occasionally, very occasionally, he felt constrained to reciprocate these civilities. The director was very bitter about the fact that he did not hold this privileged position as he rated himself just as highly as the collector, and by virtue of his work, he was accustomed to being the centre of attention.

Once or twice a year the group organised excursions. Summer, winter, it made no difference as long as everybody was available. The trips were not typical tourist fare. Although they often covered thousands of miles, ending up in implausibly distant lands, they were quite capable of returning without seeing a single sight, without strolling down a single street, without entering a single shop – regardless of whether it was their first visit. The purpose of these trips was not to see the world but to spend time together in a strange place. Each trip was planned around a particular theme, which could be as simple as reading a book, exploring a certain topic or meeting somebody. The theme, whatever it was, determined every last detail about the trip: where they stayed, what they did. This might mean that they spent the entire stay shut away in their hotel rooms, or else in the trenches of some rain-drenched archaeological site, or else in the gardens of some dilapidated mansion. It was at times like these that you could see, you could clearly see, just how close-knit this group was, and how everybody's second side shone through, displacing individual traits and characteristics. This ensemble of five moved about, sorted out obligations and dealt with minor difficulties without the least confusion, the opposite of what usually goes on in a group of friends. I didn't just have Paraschis's word for it – I saw it for myself.

I could talk about them for hours.

These people gave off a peculiar aura, especially when they were together. Sitting next to them, you could almost feel them sucking the life-blood out of you through invisible tubes. Wherever you looked, you'd fall on looks and expressions suggesting that their owners were covertly examining you, taking an X-ray of you. If you had something to say and at that moment one of them started talking (the usual butting in), they would always pause and hand back to you. It wasn't, as you might be forgiven for thinking, a matter of common courtesy. No. What was important to them was to suck you in and listen to whatever it was you had to say. They hadn't the least interest in expressing their own opinions.

One day, for example, I hurt my ankle and put one of those small adhesive plasters on it. While we were talking, I noticed the director looking down at the small swelling inside my sock – I was sitting with one leg crossed over the other which hitched the top trouser leg up a little. He didn't say anything but the actress, who was clearly following him, suddenly asked me if I'd hurt myself. Nothing escaped them. With stolen glances they had instant communication about everything. Even when their eyes narrowed into a smile, you could not shake off the feeling that behind it, their round pupils were still busily sizing you up. Even when I was miles away from them, or on the bus, I could feel their eyes boring holes right through me.

I was to be at their beck and call for an entire fortnight. That was the agreement. I was to be their guest. Our 'sessions' were mostly held at the hotel (more of which later); but there were meetings at other locations too. Actually, it might make sense to talk about the hotel now.

The hotel was on a central street. At first you don't even realise that there is a hotel there; I'm sure everybody, and I mean everybody, walks past it without noticing it. An old building, nothing special, but its position was fantastic, and that's why some very shrewd people bought up the entire ground floor, restored it, and opened two restaurants there. Two restaurants and a bar. They did very well. They were always packed. Bright lights, noise, people. Even so, it never occurred to you to try and see what was on the floor above. If you did chance to stand back a little and look up, all you'd see was a dark, slightly menacing mass, the necessary extension of the floor beneath. It was long and narrow like a railway carriage with tiny little balconies sticking out. But even so, I'm sure you'd never suspect it was a hotel. It was, the Aino hotel. The entrance gave onto a side alleyway where you'd find the sign bearing the hotel's name on a wall; so dirty that you could hardly make out the letters. You went in, then crossed an airless courtyard past the back of the restaurants which led to the lobby.

The rooms were upstairs, eight in all. Only two of them had *en suite* bathrooms. There were two further bathrooms, communal, one for every three rooms. The hotel is still there – at least I think it is. I doubt they've changed anything. The first time I walked into the courtyard, full of empty bottles and crates that the restaurants dumped round the back, I felt immediately let down by the aesthetic standards of the group. The reception area was worse: scuffed linoleum covering the floor, a cash desk, wooden panelling and peeling varnish. A young man about my age with a red earring was manning the desk and shot me a look somewhere between indifference and disparagement.

I spent a fortnight there, in one of the two luxury rooms complete with *en suite* bathroom. Another two rooms had been booked for the same period, used by different members of the group at different times. We'd taken over almost half the hotel! Paraschis and Halkiolakis spent most nights there; the other two, the couple, one or two nights. (Argyriadis was another story.) Anyway, the rooms were clean and well maintained, the plumbing seemed fairly new. Contrary to first impressions, the place was not in the least neglected. Even the wallpaper, small blue flowers on a white background, seemed to have been newly hung. It occurred to me that a few decades back, the hotel might have been quite well known in certain wealthy circles and might have been used for illicit purposes. The sheets and furniture certainly did not give the impression of being cheap. Hotels tend to operate the other way, trying to pass off fake fittings as the height of luxury. The Aino was understated throughout; when I opened the wardrobe to hang up my clothes, for instance, I found all the shelves had been lined with scented paper.

There had been the odd meeting before I settled in the hotel. Although nobody said as much, I had the impression that this was some kind of probationary period. They wanted to put me at ease, but given the company I was in, that was probably expecting too much. They showed me photograph after photograph: the photographer pictures from her various exhibitions, the actress pictures from various productions she'd been in, the director pictures from his various films, and the collector pictures of various antiques. The goldsmith was the only one who did not show me pictures. He read me poems instead. His own poems. Simos Skouris wrote. Poems and short prose pieces. I suspect he started writing after he met Chryssovergis. He did it to compensate for the disadvantage he was at relative to his wife and the rest of the group. As for whether it was any good or not, I really can't pretend to know; it was all so obscure that it was impossible to form any opinion of it whatsoever. The actress was clearly very proud of her husband's work. Anyway, she talked about it with great enthusiasm and fired everybody else up too, and even if they did not share her passion, they responded in the same vein.

My first contact with the sect (as I liked to call them) took place as I was leaving a lecture room at the university. A woman approached me. It was Tina Paraschis. I heard her say my name and ask me to confirm that I was who she thought I was. When I did, she asked if we could sit and talk somewhere quiet. I told her I was in a hurry and that two of my fellow students were waiting for me. She looked disappointed. I asked her what it was about. Instead of answering, she asked when I would be free. I said I had no idea; as she was reluctant to be specific, I decided I was too. She tore a corner off the newspaper she was carrying and jotted down her phone number. And her name. She told me to call her whenever I had time to see her.

At the time I couldn't have known what she wanted from me. I had a hunch that it had something to do with my appearance on a TV quiz game in which I managed to answer a lot of questions, beating my three opponents into the final. I thought it might be that, because a lot of people, strangers in the street, would come up to me and congratulate me. On any other occasion I would have been totally baffled by Tina Paraschis approaching me like that. But I was right – it was my TV appearance that had made her seek me out.

I called her later that afternoon. She seemed surprised to hear from me and told me so when we met.

'Naturally, I was curious,' I said. 'I enjoy digging beneath the surface.'

'That's probably something to do with your decision to become an archaeologist.'

We agreed to meet at a café. The conversation immediately turned to the subject of the TV game. Two things had made an impression on her: I answered without any hesitation about the meaning of *Phi Beta Kappa*, leaving the other contestants – a middle-aged literature graduate and a retired lawyer – looking lost alongside my unsmiling face.

'Had you heard of *Phi Beta Kappa*?'

'No!' she thrilled, as though to say 'Yes, of course!' Her enthusiasm derived from the fact that I happened to know what it was.

I asked her how she had found me. Simple; she had gathered that I was a fourth-year archaeology student, so she went along to the faculty, looked at the list of students, consulted the timetable, saw what lecture room I'd be in and waited outside. After the preliminaries, it was time for me to find out what exactly she wanted. But the noise, the people and the traffic flying past bothered her. She suggested we go back to her place; it was close by. That's what we did. Once there, she came to the point, and gave me a very detailed explanation indeed.

two

The funny thing was that the two points that had really impressed her about me were totally coincidental. The reason why I never once smiled during the show was that two days earlier the dentist had filed down one of my molars. The day they recorded the show I was standing there, with half a tooth anxiously waiting to receive its porcelain crown – the first one to install itself inside my twenty-one-year-old mouth, something I viewed at the time as a great defeat. Of course it is possible to smile without opening your mouth, but I was so anxious about accidentally revealing the gap that I unconsciously froze the expression on my face so much that it looked like I was wearing a rigid mask. That image, coupled with the apparent ease with which I answered the questions, gave the impression of a very cool contestant who had gone to the studio determined to win. But it was all purely coincidental.

The *Phi Beta Kappa* thing was a stroke of luck. Only the week before, desperate for some facts to pad out an essay on Ancient Phigalia and its famous temple of Apollo, I was burrowing through my friend's encyclopaedia when my eye fell on an entry a bit higher up on the same page in Greek script: 'Φί Βήτα Κάππα'. That's how I found out all about the fraternity of American intellectuals founded at the end of the 18th century. It was fresh in my mind, and if I had been in the mood, I could have dazzled them with my in-depth knowledge on the subject. I remembered that it stood for '*Philosophia Biou Kybernitis*' – 'The love of knowledge, the guide to life'; I could even remember their emblem – a golden key with the initials '**ΦBK**' engraved on it.

Those two coincidences, the serendipitous encyclopaedia research and my filed-down molar, had brought me the photographer, Tina Paraschis and shortly afterwards, the entire group. While we sat in her house, I realised that it was not only the noise that had prevented her from getting to the point sooner; she was embarrassed and with reason, because what she had to say was rather odd. She began by telling me how fortunate and privileged she felt in regard to those people whom fate (she actually used the word fate) had made her friends. She said a couple of words about each of

The emblem: 'ΦBK'

them and explained how they had met. Brief summaries, but it all took time.

She sensed my confusion, or at least suspected it, and tried to prepare me.

'What I am about to tell you concerns all of us – my friends.'

This comment left me none the wiser, but then she became more specific.

'If you think about it, all five of us have people-centred jobs. You might argue that all jobs are people-centred, and you'd be right, but we all work with people as our raw material. I'm a photographer. I do landscapes, buildings and life drawings too, but mostly people. That's what really fascinates me, what fascinates the majority of photographers, now that I come to think about it.'

For a moment there I thought she was going to ask to take my picture. I was wrong.

'The same goes for Ioanna the actress and Petros the director and Simos, who writes. They work with people. They bring together different elements from real people and with them create something new of their own. "The human being is the great book we must all devote our lives to reading."' That was one of Argyriadis's favourite sayings.

I objected that Argyriadis's line of business, antiques, was hardly anthropocentric in the same way.

'Yes, that's right, but then again, nothing absorbs him more than the observation and study of human characteristics. The problem is that in this day and age, with everything going on around us, we are losing many of the features that make us worthy of attention. You see people in the street and they look positively dehydrated, no spirit, no breath in them. It's a rare thing to come across someone who reminds you of the divine origins of the species. When I saw you on television, I felt enormously relieved – I mean it; there is hope, I thought.'

I was beginning to get the picture, but hadn't a clue where this was all leading, and have to admit to being totally stunned. And confused: what she was saying, effectively, was that because there is a shortage of noteworthy people these days, and because I seemed to them to be interesting at some point (something which I have explained was sheer chance), we should do what? Become bosom buddies all of a sudden? Let them take me under their wing? Those thoughts made me uncomfortable. I hadn't the least desire to join their 'Order of Very Strange People' – however flattering the offer was from one perspective. Besides, the age gap of two and a half decades complicated the whole thing further.

I was overwhelmed by the urge to tell her that if I had taken part in the quiz just one week earlier, I would have been at a loss to answer any questions about *Phi Beta Kappa* and, moreover, would most likely have been smiling benignly throughout the show. The retired lawyer would have won, and Tina Paraschis would barely have registered my existence. All I had to do was tell her that; I'd tell her that and instantly extricate myself from this awkward situation. But she stopped me and I said nothing until she finished; if I had spoken, I wouldn't have heard the rest.

'We keep our eyes peeled. We are always on the look out for exceptions. For special people who would be interesting to meet, and getting to know them enables us to study yet another chapter in that great book called The Human Being.'

I'm not sure whether those were her precise words, but there was definitely something poetic about them. I looked at her questioningly and asked (it was now obvious where the conversation was headed) how she could be sure that I did in fact belong to their category of the exceptional. She smiled and without another word, without giving me an answer, came to the heart of the matter.

The first step would be for me to meet the other four. After that we would be able to make an agreement. For my part, I would have to give them some of my time, a few days they could use for the purpose of 'investigating' me. I would be at their disposal, for discussions, for questioning, for short walks and visits, and anything else they might need. All of this would be carried out with the greatest tact and discretion, and would not at any point be allowed to weary or irritate me. I looked at her without saying a word – the truth is that at that moment my brain had stopped working altogether.

'It'll be quite painless,' she said in an appealing voice. 'We're not cannibals or anything. You'll enjoy it.'

She told me about the hotel. She told me that it would be a good idea if I booked into the same hotel as them so we'd have a common base. Alternatively, we could arrange a short trip, but it wasn't a good time for anyone to get away. She had picked up momentum and was talking a lot. They would draw up a schedule of group meetings as well as private meetings with individual members of the group, working around everybody's schedule. After that, they'd have to decide whether they would need an extension for further sessions. She spoke as though she took my cooperation for granted. I could tell from the way she talked, so self-possessed, so articulate and so completely oblivious to my own state of shock, that this was not the first time she had made this kind of arrangement.

I would be paid for my participation in the program. There's no point in mentioning the exact sum because it was eight years ago and the figure is therefore quite meaningless; suffice it to say that it covered five months' rent on my small flat in the centre of town. The prospect of having five months' rent money in my pocket had an instant effect on me – call me cheap, call me self-interested, but it's the truth. This new factor overrode my embarrassment and shock and put paid to all my reservations. Money is an effective motivator: I was suddenly fired up and ready to accept on the spot. In only minutes, I had executed a deft *volte face*, and was now scared that she might change her mind. Paraschis herself pre-empted any commitment from me.

'Think it over for a day or two – meet the others first, then give us your answer.'

This was followed by the preliminary meetings I mentioned before. Three, perhaps four, short meetings. When I finally gave Paraschis my answer, I could tell she wasn't at all surprised. Later I was given the dates for the fortnight when I was to be at the disposal of the group, the dates I would be staying at the Aino.

That was eight years ago. It's a pity that I didn't write all this down earlier; some details will have slipped my memory. Then again, perhaps not. Sometimes I think everything is still there intact, inside my head in hair-raising detail. But I wonder if that will still be the case ten or twenty years hence. The song that's on at the moment was a huge hit back then. I'm watching the cassette as it plays, observing it as it wraps itself around the spool. At first I follow it with my eyes, but after a while my mind takes over. The tape unwinds, vanishes briefly into the darkness of the cassette player and re-emerges on the opposite spool to continue its journey. In much the same way I did during that fortnight – that's exactly how I got caught up in their machinations. They stuffed me in, chewed me up and waited for me to come out the other side.

tHRee

The young man with the red earring I'd seen when I entered
the hotel was there again in the evening. Because I was
sure that he'd looked askance at me earlier, which I didn't
appreciate at all, I deliberately struck up a conversation with
him, on the pretext of finding out about local bus routes.
He told me he was the son of the fat man with the moles all
over his face who was outside watering the trees, and that he
helped out whenever he was needed. From what I gathered,
there was no mother; father and son lived alone in a large
ground floor room. At first I thought the hotel belonged to
them, but it didn't. They just worked there. Apart from them,
I saw two cleaners and two chambermaids who worked on
a rota. They didn't need any more staff than that. Stelios,
the one with the earring, took care of all errands, shopping
and so on – whatever his father needed doing. He didn't
give the impression that he took the initiative much, or was
that hard working. But if you made the effort to be friendly,
he'd happily sit and chat for hours. I found out quite a lot
from Stelios, so much that his father warned him not to get
too chatty with me. It was strange but from the moment I
arrived I had the sense of foreboding that one day I would be
reading about his untimely end in the newspaper: that he'd

be killed after drunk-driving, or arrested on arms smuggling charges or drowned in some shipwreck. I don't know why but I had a bad feeling about him. So far I have read nothing of the kind about Stelios. Not yet.

Stelios was in fact very perceptive. He would tell me things that would turn out to be absolutely right. One good thing about him though was that he never hesitated to speak his mind about anybody. He'd never break a confidence; if he knew that he was supposed to keep quiet about something, he was totally unreachable. I'll never forget the look on his face the first time I mentioned the actress. 'She's crazy!' I realised that by 'crazy' he wasn't trying to imply that she was deranged in any sense; his comment worked at a deeper level, suggesting that something about her was profoundly irritating, a feeling I had no trouble identifying with. But the way he said it was so disarming. I envied him that. I'm forever checking myself, and have a hard time saying what I really think. If his father had caught him saying that, he'd have been in big trouble. You can be sure of that. Basically, Stelios couldn't stand anyone in the group – with the exception of Argyriadis, naturally – which explains why he gave me that look when I arrived at the hotel as their guest.

I met Ioanna Chryssovergis on one of my first nights at the Aino. It was late – must have been after midnight. That in itself was not proof of her eccentricity; she was in a play at the time and we could only meet after the performance because she slept during the day. I should explain that every day, every morning, I'd find a piece of paper slipped under my door setting out the day's programme, who I was to see at what time. Thankfully, before my meeting with the actress, I'd had plenty of time to myself; I'd seen her husband several hours earlier (I'll write about him some other time) and so I had the chance to sleep a bit beforehand. I'm sure it didn't occur to any of them that a 1 am meeting might be a bit late for me. It seems that they took it for granted that everyone went to bed after four and got up late. Argyriadis was the only exception; I had the impression that the man never slept at all.

I had never heard of Ioanna Chryssovergis; that doesn't mean that she wasn't a decent, respected actress; it's just that I was not a theatre lover, never had been, and had no idea who was who. When I say that I'd never heard of her, I do so for one reason alone – to make it clear that I neither admired her nor felt the kind of awe you feel when you come face to face with someone you have only ever known from a distance.

Let me go back to that night. I heard but didn't quite register Chryssovergis's first knock on my door, dazed with exhaustion as I was. It took a second knock to get me on my feet to open the door.

When she walked into my room, I had the strange feeling that we'd never met. Her expression had changed completely from the one I was accustomed to from the group sessions, perhaps because this time we were alone, or at least without the others. I have already mentioned how odd it was when they all got together. She now gave the impression of being unconscionably arrogant, trying at every turn to make me feel that her visit was a gift from above. Her face looked different too – more pointy, with an off-putting harshness. It suddenly became clear to me what had brought on this change; she clearly felt insecure within the group and struggled to maintain her position in an undeclared hierarchy. The effort it took made her appear full of energy, radiant even. But alone with me, she felt securely ensconced on her throne and there was nobody threatening to depose her. Her innate superiority she took for granted, as well as the understanding that I would bow uncritically before her. The message was unambiguous: she and I were not equals.

She had no desire to waste time on me. I suspect that deep down she found all this business about the proper study of mankind rather tiresome, but probably reckoned that she might as well list some of her virtues while she was at it. I remember how emphatically she spoke and how fired up she was on the subject of her supreme talent, her effortless way of winning people over through her charm mechanism.

'When you are in control of this mechanism, it happens automatically. At the flick of a switch, it is set in motion. You wrap yourself up inside a cloud, which other people find irresistible. The locks burst open, the doors swing back, and you just breeze in and win them over. You don't have to be polite, clever, or charming. Just a flick of the switch, that's all it takes, and everybody surrenders to you. This is why I'm so good at acting; there's nothing else to it. I discovered the mechanism. It's as simple as that. And very useful; a great help. Everything else falls into place after that.'

I remained strangely invulnerable to her charms. In fact, I found her presence quite irksome. So what was going wrong with this fail safe mechanism of hers – why wasn't it working on me? Perhaps she'd forgotten that crucial flick of the switch. Stelios found her just as irritating as I did, maybe more so.

The woman was utterly mad. I remember saying that to myself, thinking that all that business about the charm mechanism might have been something she'd heard somewhere, had liked the sound of, and tried to pass off as her own. Or perhaps it was wishful thinking? Who knows?

She must have stayed for about an hour, an hour and a half. I don't remember much else about the occasion. The main thing about that evening wasn't my meeting with the actress but what took place directly afterwards.

four

As soon as Chryssovergis left, I flopped into bed but couldn't sleep. There was nothing unusual about that: sleep is never around when you need it and impossible to get rid of when you don't.

I went downstairs in the hope of finding Stelios. I had seen him earlier that night sitting alone in the makeshift seating area next to the reception desk. I was in a mood to exercise my tongue and I knew that the actress was Stelios's pet topic. But he wasn't there, so although I wasn't at all sleepy, I went back to my room.

It wasn't just that I was wakeful; I was insanely tense with all my senses working overtime, like an animal trying to elude the hunt. Perhaps it was thanks to this unnatural vigilance that I spotted, for the first time, right at the end of the corridor and a few metres along from my room, an open doorway with a doorframe that did not appear to have a door in it. There were no other doors on this side of the corridor, just a window looking onto an enormous plane tree sprouting its first leaves.

I was familiar with the layout of the floor; I knew where all the other rooms were, where the shared bathrooms were, and couldn't understand how I had missed that doorway, especially since it wasn't out of sight or in some dark corner. Perhaps it was the light, the way the dimly lit corridor, in combination with the whiteish light projected from the window, made the narrow opening stand out against its frame. Our powers of observation are frequently at the mercy of tricks of light.

As I came closer, I noticed that there was a staircase leading up from the doorway – it only went up, so there was obviously another floor! I climbed it and found myself standing in front of a closed door. There was no other door there, so I concluded that it must lead up to some kind of small lumber-room on the terrace. That's why you couldn't see anything from below. I imagined that they used it as a storeroom or linen cupboard, and had some pieces of old junk stashed away in there too. I made a note to ask Stelios about it in the morning. I assumed it was locked, but turned the knob half-heartedly anyway.

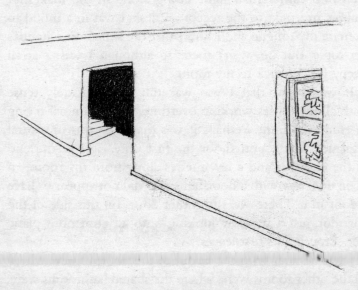

Dark passage with stairs

I was wrong. As soon as I touched it, the door retreated on its hinges, revealing an illuminated room. The first things I noticed were two heavy jet-black plant stands, and the side panel of a large desk. Then a body sitting at the desk – I say body because the head was concealed by a large number of books piled up on top of the desk. I stood there stunned, the doorknob still grasped tightly in my hand. The minute I recovered my senses, I started to close the door, very warily, so I could slip away unnoticed, but I stopped myself; it occurred to me how embarrassing it would be if the body behind the books suddenly spotted me trying to escape down the stairs like a thief.

So, with all the confidence of someone who knows he has nothing to hide, I pushed the door back again, and said in a calm and steady voice:

'Excuse me, sir. Forgive me for disturbing you. I accidentally opened your door.'

five

That was when I saw a head emerging from behind the books. It turned to look in my direction, and from that look, still absorbed in what he had been reading, I recognised the eyes of the collector. He didn't seem at all thrown by my sudden appearance, and was quick to respond to my own discomfort.

'Ah! Our young archaeologist,' he said warmly, 'who, it seems, has decided to dabble in exploration! Come in. Come in. What a shame I've deprived you of the thrill of thinking you'd stumbled across a secret chamber. This is just a room, my room. No mystery attached to it, I'm afraid.'

I remember giving him a very clever answer.

'I have discovered a secret chamber. A secret is not only something that nobody else knows, but everything we are ignorant of until the moment we discover it. I, for instance, was unaware that there was a staircase here.'

'That happens to a lot of people. A staircase in a doorway no one ever notices.'

The same could be said for the hotel in general.

Let me describe the room. A large, square room so full of clutter there was hardly anywhere to stand. The walls were lined with shelves from floor to ceiling, all heaving with books. There were even shelves above the lintel. There was a small reddish-brown sofa – that too was so full of stuff that it was almost completely concealed. Exquisite paintings. A female nude mounted in an old engraved frame. A forest, and another work showing three male figures. The only thing in the room that wasn't underneath something else was the desk chair. There was another armchair, upholstered in a deep yellow-gold fabric with a colossal paraffin lamp in its embrace. He told me to move the lamp and sit down, but in my efforts to do so I discovered that the lamp was too heavy to lift. It was an old ship's lantern. A little bit further to the side was an old oak bed, unmade. All this disarray was bathed in a soft, pervasive yellow light which seemed to mark off the room from the outside world and created the impression that you were shut away in a separate sphere, forging a solitary path through the darkness of space.

He asked me if I'd had my scheduled meeting with Chryssovergis. I had to restrain myself from voicing the distaste she had provoked in me.

'Don't allow yourself to be misled. Don't jump to any conclusions about her.'

I took on board what he said. I'm not sure what was behind these words; perhaps he had wrongly assumed that I had fallen for the actress's charms and was trying to give me a friendly warning or, alternatively, had sensed my lack of enthusiasm and was asking me to keep an open mind. I couldn't understand what this misleading impression might be, but said nothing, and he quickly jumped back to the beginning of our conversation.

'Imagine if this room really had been a secret chamber – how much more exciting it would have been for you – if, for example, the staircase you found had been concealed by a tall piece of furniture or a curtain. If you'd realised that there was a concerted effort to keep this space secret, and even if the room was empty – utterly empty – you would have been delighted with your discovery even so.'

I wanted to smile but then remembered that what they had so admired about me was my unsmiling face so I remained serious.

'The discovery of a secret is always more beguiling than the secret itself. Say you come across – for argument's sake – a torn letter, shredded into small pieces. You painstakingly reassemble it and read it. That's the beauty of it. The insignificant details contained in those fragments, "what I did during my holidays", "how your son performed in his exams" are of no interest to you. The essence lies in the stolen glance, wouldn't you agree?'

I did.

'You know, I have a natural abhorrence for birds. Any kind of fowl. There's nothing I can do about it; it's an ingrained disgust, a feeling of revulsion mixed with fear. I don't pay it much attention, and don't try to hide it, all my friends are aware of this idiosyncrasy of mine. Now, had I presented it to you differently, as a sore point, something I went to great lengths to conceal, if I had made you swear that you'd never tell anyone about it, you would automatically have been flattered and grateful for the trust I'd shown you by confiding this superficially insignificant detail in you. Think about the art of the novel, hasn't the novel always exploited the potential of the secret? An author, rather than giving away the secret from the outset, keeps it concealed behind a number of veils and makes the reader lift them one by one to experience the pleasure of peeling back the many layers of mystery and finally unearthing the secret. Because if we're honest, we all relish the excitement of playing detective, something those shrewd old authors knew only too well.'

It didn't take much to launch Argyriadis into a monologue. I noticed that his voice started off calm and hoarse, and if nothing disturbed his line of thought, after a while he would break into an unbridled gallop. He became more voluble, his words jostling for position, and his gestures becoming wilder, as though he were giving a public lecture. Stelios, half-jokingly, had nicknamed him the 'orator'. The most arresting thing about it was that as he neared the climax, the natural hoarseness of his voice receded, as though it had rediscovered its lost timbre and its bell-like ring.

But this monologue had not come to an end.

'Our secrets are our treasure troves. Imagine a man who has no secrets: everybody knows everything there is to know about him; no mystery there. He is faceless. An open book. That painting,' he broke off to point to the picture of the three male figures, 'has perspective.' He was pointing straight at the stone ruin visible behind them. 'An event from the past, a piece of information, something about ourselves, everything we keep hidden from others, this is the perspective on the canvas of our lives, the one thing that lends us depth.'

I was only twenty-one years old. That might have been why I started to feel so uncomfortable each time Filippos Argyriadis developed his ideas in this way. I felt that I was being used as a paid audience, obliged to sit and listen – much as I had felt with Chryssovergis. That was just a piece of idiocy on my part; I would have done well to listen to him with greater care. The arrogance of youth defined my attitude to everyone and everything.

The honey-tinted light of the room made me drowsy. I continued to listen to his voice, which had grown hoarse once more. Now he was dealing with secret codes of communication and cryptography. Apparently he noticed that my eyelids had grown heavy – even though I could swear they never once closed on me – and suggested I go to take a rest.

'So, tonight you discovered where my room is, something the others have known for a long time. Don't worry. The Aino has other genuinely secret places awaiting discovery.'

I assumed he was speaking metaphorically. I restored the lamp to the embrace of the armchair.

'The seats in this room are useless,' he said, 'I do not receive visitors here. Each time you come, you'll have to move that lamp – that's if you need to sit down at all.'

I told him that it was fine by me, and in my desire to establish a tone of familiarity between us (fool!), I told him there was no need for him to address me in the formal plural form. He swung round and looked at me in astonishment, clearly irritated. With a stern expression he explained to me that he would use the familiar singular form with me if and when he saw fit. This disastrous initiative left me humiliated, but he obviously felt that the matter was closed and with an inscrutable smile (the significance of which I was not to fathom until much later) he took me by the elbow and said, 'As a student of archaeology, you are naturally familiar with all the available material concerning the mythical Aino, are you not?'

This question rescued me from one awkward situation only to send me hurtling into another, even more awkward situation, because it was only then that it dawned on me that the name Aino meant absolutely nothing to me. The charisma of the wise young man which I had been flaunting all this time was suddenly under threat. Nevertheless, I smiled, nodding my head as though in agreement.

'But you're tired now. We'll leave Aino for another time, shall we?' he said, offering me an escape route.

I charged down the stairs, practically stumbling, resolved to get my hands on everything I could find concerning Aino As for the issue of formal and familiar address, all I can say is that Filippos Argyriadis never once addressed me in the familiar form.

SIX

I was up early the next day, hoping to take advantage of the few free hours I had. I wanted to go down to the centre of town, to the faculty library, to research Aino. On my way out, I bumped into Stelios and we got talking, which delayed me, but was not altogether a waste of time as I found out a lot about the bizarre hotel from him.

I filled him in on the events of the night before, how I had stumbled across Filippos Argyriadis in his room. It was the first – and perhaps the only – time I saw Stelios laugh so much. He found the whole thing outrageous, but was surprised that I hadn't known where Argyriadis's room was. How could I have known? And there was something else I did not know, something more important: the owner of the Aino was none other than Filippos Argyriadis.

His father had left it to him, about twelve years before. Back then, there weren't any bars or restaurants on the ground floor, and the entire building was used as a hotel. Back then it was called Hotel Phoenix. When Filippos Argyriadis inherited it, the neighbourhood had already undergone some significant changes. Property prices had soared, shopping centres and exclusive boutiques were popping up everywhere, and land as a result was hard to find and harder to afford, particularly on a central street such as the one the Phoenix looked onto. The collector, with his shrewd sense, (which I believe defines him) was not slow to appreciate the commercial potential of the building, and quickly sold off the ground floor for a princely sum, keeping on the upper floor as a hotel and changing its name from Phoenix to Aino.

Stelios's father (I cannot for the life of me remember his name) arrived and joined in the conversation. He had started work at the Phoenix when he was fifteen, as an apprentice to Argyriadis's father. He was one of those people who love to talk about the old days and whenever they find themselves with a captive audience, would spare them no detail. I was something more than a passive victim; there were things I wanted to know.

The hotel was built shortly before the outbreak of World War II. It had always operated as a hotel. At that time, these areas were almost completely uninhabited, with the exception of the beehives and the odd rehabilitation clinic for consumptives taking advantage of the excellent climate. This was the rationale for opening a hotel in the area; relatives planning more than a short visit to their loved ones would inevitably descend on the Phoenix. Shortly thereafter the building was requisitioned by the Germans for the duration of the war, and afterwards resumed operation. But what role Argyriadis senior played during the Occupation remains muddy; at least that's what I surmised from some of the things Stelios began to say before he was cut off by his father's furious glances, which only fuelled my suspicions. I can't recall his precise words, but I was left with the impression that he had been an informer or a blackmarketeer, or something or the kind.

With the Germans and the consumptives gone, the hotel began to fall into disrepair. That was when Stelios's father started working there, so all the information he gave me about those years was first-hand. Their clientele gradually became restricted to couples of all descriptions, both illicit and licit, but he was anxious to stress that they were always quality people.

'Our guests were respectable people. The old man never allowed the place to deteriorate into a bordello. His prices were too high for that and he kept the riff-raff out that way. Besides, what was he supposed to say? No, you can't have a room? There were also the occasional family and travellers – the motorway exit's only a few minutes from here, but it was really couples for the most part. Semi-legitimate you might say. And the place was a bit out of the way. I got to see all sorts then. Nothing would surprise me any more. I was a young man and found it all very entertaining. A bit of an education. My most important lesson was how to keep my mouth shut. Basic principle. Been trying to drum it into his thick skull.' He motioned to Stelios, 'See no evil, hear no evil, speak no evil.'

'Then the building began to fall apart; Argyriadis didn't spend much on preservatives.' (Stelios's father had an impressive range of malapropisms.) 'The place went to seed and people stopped coming. Then he started a huge rebuilding operation that lasted the full seven years.' I thought he meant that the refurbishment took seven years but he was in fact referring to the seven-year dictatorship of the colonels. 'The old man had powerful connections, got a loan, and the hotel was soon as good as new: Phoenix by name, phoenix by nature.'

It struck me as odd that the same man, who only a few minutes earlier had looked daggers at his son for being indiscreet about his late employer's dubious relationship with the Occupation forces, was now openly declaring his dubious connections with the Junta. I could only conclude that he did not consider the latter to be quite so reprehensible – there was nothing disparaging in his tone to suggest he did.

'The old man died in '79, poor chap. The following year Filippos Argyriadis carried out his own repairs to the upper floor. More or less gutted the place; ripped out almost everything the old man had put in down to the last tiles, beautiful tiles they were, shiny olive green and orange with matching sanitary ware. The curtains came down, new curtains they were, I remember them – lovely woven beige curtains. And the beds, beautiful, comfortable beds with solid formica headboards, indestructible stuff formica – he pulled out the lot of it and imported tiles from Italy. Everything you see upstairs is old, all of it. He went round all the architectural salvage yards picking up stuff from the 30s and 40s, the same age as the building. You'd never catch me throwing money after old junk, but everyone's different, aren't they? The bottom line is that old things are his line of work and he knows what he's doing. He is a collector, after all.'

'And an orator,' muttered Stelios under his breath, smirking away.

'That's enough. You've crossed the line this time. That's the difference between you and this gentleman – one look at the company you keep and one look at the company he keeps, says it all. You're really getting on my nerves today.'

Stelios wasn't listening. He was pretending to look out of the window.

'He brought in old pieces of furniture too. If you take the trouble to look, you'll see that no two rooms are the same. Different furniture in each one. Some of the pieces were originals from the early days of the Phoenix. Some others are from his collection. The man's got a true Minus touch.' I think the reference must have been to the Phrygian king, but I let it go. 'It's only down here, reception and the lobby, that he left alone. Every year he says he's going to decorate but he never gets round to it. Maybe he's used to having it like this; if you ask me, it'll stay like this forever and a day.'

I asked whether the place attracted enough guests to keep going. The answer was categorical. The Aino is always full. It may not get tourists or passing custom, but it's a regular meeting place for several businessmen and professionals from the provinces, who would never give up their refuge in the capital. According to him, one of these businessmen, only last night, had complained that his favourite room, Room 8, my room that is, was unavailable. Seizing the opportunity, he started to describe the particular habits of each of these regulars; if I hadn't interrupted him, he would have gone on until noon. But I was in a hurry, and set off for the library.

seven

I'm jumping from subject to subject, I know. There is no logical sequence to my narrative. But there are times when certain thoughts invade your head, forcing you to attend to them right away. Ignore them, and you risk losing them forever.

A short while ago, as I was leafing through this notebook, my eye fell on a word I used earlier – hierarchy. It is easy for anyone to see that within the sect a ranking system was in operation, a scale where everyone was positioned, on a lower or a higher rung relative to everyone else. It was even obvious, at least to me, who occupied the top rung and who was at the bottom. Filippos Argyriadis was the undisputed head, and Simos Skouris was on the lowest rung. It was not at all clear, however, what the placing in between looked like. By observing certain details, I managed to come up with this list, which I think adequately reflects the group hierarchy as it stood at the time:

- Filippos Argyriadis, first.
- Petros Halkiolakis, second place.
- Ioanna Chryssovergis, third place.
- Tina Paraschis, fourth place.
- Simos Skouris, last.

Argyriadis, as much as Skouris, had a distinctive calm about him. What I mean is that both men were totally indifferent to their ranking, and did not really care if the situation were to change. The other three, conversely, were in a state of perpetual competition, subliminal and implacable, struggling either to maintain their position or to improve it.

Chryssovergis for instance, like I said, adored Argyriadis, was frequently sarcastic to Halkiolakis and would put Paraschis down. Paraschis got on well with everybody apart from the actress. The director, for his part, on the one hand couldn't care less about Chryssovergis but on the other was bothered that he was not at the top. (I am sure that it never once occurred to them while they were observing me that I was studying them just as carefully.)

I came to realise later that the complexities of their relationships influenced how they behaved towards me. I was Paraschis's discovery. It was Paraschis who had spotted me; it was Paraschis who had sought me out; it was Paraschis who had approached me and introduced me to the group. If I managed to create a favourable impression on the rest of the group, the photographer's star would automatically rise, irritating Chryssovergis during its ascent. This is perhaps explanation enough as to why she had been so negative towards me, particularly on the occasion when we met alone. Now, in contrast, you would often hear Halkiolakis singing my praises, quite deliberately calculated to annoy Chryssovergis.

I, an outsider, who had not been among them for long, managed to draw quite a number of conclusions and, to a certain extent, decode the way in which they acted and reacted. And I wonder, were they, the players in this game, conscious at every turn of the reasons why they moved their pieces this way and not that way? Were the rules of the game known to all and agreed on by all? I think not. Not one of them would confess to harbouring feelings of jealousy – much less admit that these feelings guided their behaviour. (If there was anything the group was proud of, it was the appearance of coherence, the smooth facade visible to the outside world.) I believe it was something unconscious, like the instinctive struggle of a pack of hounds seeing which one of them would assert itself at the head of the pack and the rest in their serried ranks.

And something else: I frequently refer to them by profession (actor, collector, etc.) rather than name. It's a habit I picked up from them. Naturally, they were on first name terms, but whenever reference was made to an absent member of the group, the professional designation was always preferred: 'Our director is a little late today,' or 'Why don't we consult our photographer first?' Profession, preceded by a statutory 'our'. It was a conspiratorial intimacy, a charming show of affection. Now that I have these thoughts safely down on paper, I can pick up the thread from where I left off.

My research was a waste of time. However many volumes I consulted, however painstakingly I scoured them, however recondite the references I followed, the result was the same. There was no evidence of the name Aino. Anywhere. I spent hours in the library, and even with the assistance of the most experienced archivist came up with nothing. The books stubbornly refused to yield the information I needed.

As it started to dawn on me that my struggle was fruitless, I felt something akin to an electrical charge coursing through me, leaving the hairs on my body bristling: Argyriadis had magically excised all trace of Aino to make me look foolish. (It's ridiculous, but whenever something strange and unforeseen happens, my mind always grasps for the most metaphysical explanation and only later looks for a more rational cause.) But I didn't give up. My next move would be to go to the faculty and find the man who had the answer to everything, Professor Athanasios Marneris.

I saw him leave the building and head for his car. I followed him, convinced that he would not recognise me because of his famously bad eyesight (there was some doubt as to whether he could actually make out the faces in the first two rows of the auditorium). Relying on this fact, I pretended to be one of his students to give me a pretext for talking to him.

'Please forgive me for disturbing you outside lecture time.'

'If it's important, consider yourself forgiven,' he said peering at me from behind his thick lenses, through the two slits in his face he had for eyes.

'Professor Marneris, what is known about Aino?'

I put the question to him in an upbeat, positive voice, my tone communicating the assumption that Aino did exist, and he knew all about it. The two slits widened to reveal two ailing eyeballs.

'Aino?'

'Yes.'

'*Alpha, iota, nu, omega* – feminine ending?'

'Yes.'

'Doesn't exist.'

He carried on towards his car. I stood there rooted to the spot, staring after him. After four or five steps, sensing that I was still watching him, he stopped, and turning his head just enough to make himself heard but not so much that he had to adjust his pace, 'Ainos, masculine, with an *omicron*, yes; Aineias, yes, but Aino, feminine, with an *omega*? No. Can't imagine where you got hold of such a notion.'

Without waiting for an answer, he climbed into his car. His driver had already started the engine.

eight

After the professor's response, there was only one logical conclusion: Aino was nothing more than a fabrication with a plausibly ancient ring to it, which duped the hearer into assuming a weighty classical heritage.

The only thing left was to work out what I was going to say the next time I saw Argyriadis. I felt like I had fallen victim of a carefully orchestrated farce. He had stuck an ancient-sounding name on the end of a hook, dangled it under my nose, and fool that I am, I rose to the bait.

I replayed the scene over and over in my mind. It was by now quite clear to me that the words 'you as an archaeologist will naturally be familiar with Aino' were calculated to manoeuvre me into a corner where to confess ignorance would involve a loss of face. He then granted me a period of grace, 'Why don't we leave Aino for another time?', confident that I would dash off in search of information at the first opportunity, and confident that I would return empty-handed. Now he would be anticipating the entertaining spectacle of me trying to cover my tracks and the disingenuousness in my desire to play the know-it-all.

This angered me; I'd been played for a fool. But I did remember, and this was of some consolation to me, that my only response to his question had been a silent nod. I had said nothing, nothing at all. I didn't say, 'Yes, of course I am familiar with Aino.' A simple nod, and how often do we nod in agreement to questions that we only half understand or aren't really listening to? People usually can tell the difference between a meaningful nod and a token nod, and will often repeat the question so as to avoid any future embarrassment. What I'm getting at here is, what is a nod? An unconscious, random movement. I decided to stop agonising about the matter and even ignore any further attempts on Argyriadis's part to resurrect the discussion.

I went back to the hotel. The minute I walked in, Stelios pounced on me.

'Where have you been? Why are you so late?'

I looked at the clock. It was already 3 pm, I had completely lost track of time; I was sure it was 1 pm, at the latest. My research project must have been more absorbing than I'd realised.

'Skouris has been down twice looking for you. Go on, give him a knock. He's in Room 4.'

Our appointment had been at 1.30 pm. This was the first time I was late. Spectacularly so. Simos Skouris and I had met once before, and on that occasion too there had been something so unbelievably comical in the air that I kept wanting to laugh.

He was sitting opposite me in an armchair, and opened a large ledger, like the ones used by accountants in the old days. He was busy taking notes on all manner of things about me that he considered important: my family's voting habits, whether I had brothers and sister, younger or older, my favourite food. I couldn't help myself. He came across like a schoolboy trying very hard to prove how studious he is. Perhaps he was the only one to take the issue so seriously and perhaps he was struggling to prove, however belatedly, that his inclusion in the group was merited. Sometimes his questions bordered on the pseudo-intellectual, sounding like they'd been plucked from one of those self-administered psychological quizzes that women's magazine are full of. I cannot recall answering him with any sincerity more than a couple of times.

He wasn't so much annoyed by my lateness as concerned that I'd taken off for good. As soon as he saw me, he calmed down. I sat down opposite him, he opened the ledger and started going through his questions, his spectacles perched approximately half way down his nose and his bald pate radiating a reddish glow. After half an hour of questions in the manner of a doctor trying to form a picture of a new patient's medical history Skouris slammed the ledger shut, only to open it again immediately, apparently looking for something on the last pages. I saw that there were more notes at the back.

'I've been doing some research,' he said with the air of a mad professor, 'and have come across some information about that fraternity, about *Phi Beta Kappa*.'

'Here we go again,' I thought.

'*Philosophia Biou Kybernitis*. Indeed. I wasn't entirely sure if the middle word "*Biou*" referred to the preceding "*Philosophia*" or the "*Kybernitis*" that follows. What exactly does the phrase mean? Does it imply that philosophy is the guide to life or the philosophy of life is our guide? It's rather like the ancient "*arren ou thili*" which can mean "boy, not girl", or "not boy, girl" – the meaning changes according to your interpretation of "*ou*".'

We soon concluded that both versions were essentially the same, and moved on. Simos Skouris had researched the history of *Phi Beta Kappa* with the diligence of a schoolboy writing up a subject not on the curriculum.

'Let's see. Founded in 1776. Grew and flourished at

William and Mary College, the second oldest college in the U.S. Other chapters started in colleges around the country. Women not admitted for over a century. Amazing. Did you know that?'

I said I did. Even though I didn't.

'The most astonishing thing of all is that the fraternity operated under a stringent code of secrecy until 1831. Just imagine, the original members, a crew of tail-coated, behatted young men, coming together for clandestine meetings in secret, candlelit locations to discuss literature, arguing about the relative merits of various writers and poets. Positively salivating. What wouldn't I give to have been a fly on the wall at one of those early meetings. When they met, the members exchanged a secret handshake – index finger and middle finger raised up to their lips and then moving from left to right to symbolise the assurance that their lips were sealed. There was also an oath which bound them to secrecy.'

He had clearly fallen under the fraternity spell. He turned the page and went on.

'The branches at other universities started to multiply. Five quickly became twenty-five, twenty-five soon grew to 525. The number of members increased correspondingly. In 1900, when the first official membership list was published, extant members numbered 10,500. Today we are looking at about half a million. Because as you know,' (I nodded), '*Phi Beta Kappa* is not some quaint anachronism – on the contrary. Some of the wealthiest families in America have belonged to its ranks: authors, artists, politicians. Henry James, Pearl S. Buck, John Adams, Nathaniel Hawthorne, Helen Keller, Longfellow, down to Bush and Bill Clinton. Just think, it all began with five students from Virginia who met one December night in 1776 and decided to start a club.'

His eyes gleamed with inspiration. It is not impossible

47

that the thought was going through his head that their own club – also composed of five members – might evolve into something similar.

'It's the oldest and most influential organisation in America. Their emblem is a gold...'

'A golden key with the initials 'ΦΒΚ' engraved on it,' I piped up. That I did know.

He looked at me, wordlessly, and I realised that there was something on his mind and he was wondering how to phrase it.

'You may be unaware of this, but we were all extremely impressed when you, a young man, had all this knowledge at your fingertips, on a subject we knew absolutely nothing about. I won't deny that I was envious. In the positive sense, of course. Always in the positive sense. That's why I've been collecting all this information. Ha! Ha!'

He laughed. Deep down, Simos Skouris was a rather naïve character.

'If you sit down and think about it, one group of intellectuals has led you to another. Tell me, how did you come to know about *Phi Beta Kappa*?' he asked, unintentionally hitting a sore spot. I was not about to reveal the fact that it had been sheer serendipity that had led me to *Phi Beta Kappa*.

'I enjoy learning new things,' I answered vaguely. He didn't pursue the point. Perhaps in an attempt to change the subject, perhaps influenced by some other stray impulse, I heard myself ask a question which just that moment had popped into my head.

'Who came up with the name Aino?'

My question clearly disconcerted him. He looked almost guilty. After all, and I'll say this again, Simos Skouris was at heart a naïve character.

'Don't drag me into all that,' he stammered.

NINE

Aino nights – that smell…

As soon as I took Tina Paraschis up on her offer, particularly after I had moved into the hotel, I no longer saw my involvement as some great adventure; more as a task in need of completion. I tried my best to be co-operative, and at the same time maintain my new image of *'wunderkind'*. I think that what really helped me adjust to my new environment was the thought of bringing over a lot of my own things to the hotel room: my tape player, books, teddy bear (souvenir of an old love affair) and, of course, my clothes. Besides, the Aino was very comfortable.

But at night I often woke up feeling disoriented. I get this when I sleep away from home. One particular night, I opened my eyes, and saw the large wardrobe leaning against the wall opposite. I stared at it, puzzled. How had that got there? I sat up and repeated the question. Although my body was making movements and my eyes were open, I was far from awake. I struggled to work out where I was, but instead of looking around the room for clues, my gaze remained fixed on the wardrobe as if it held all the answers. Still asleep, I got out of bed, walked up to it, and opened one of its doors, convinced that behind it — unbelievable! — lay everything I needed to know. When I saw my shirts hanging there, I woke up, wondering what I was doing standing in front of an open wardrobe. I vaguely recalled that all that business about waking up in a strange room with an oak wardrobe in it must have been a dream. It was only then that I realised I was sleepwalking. I went back to bed and back to sleep.

However, these small disturbances were not the only thing that made me feel that my nights at the Aino were somehow different, somehow unusual. Once darkness fell, it was as though the entire upper floor had detached itself from the rest of the hotel and had become self-contained. Whichever window you looked out of, trees surrounded the place, the same trees whose dark forms shielded the hotel from the prying eyes of passers-by and were transformed — I'm waxing lyrical now — into a green puffy cloud with the hull of the Aino reclining on top. At least that's what it looked like. The trees were in exactly the same place as they were by day; that didn't change, but by night, with all the coloured lights from the bars and restaurants below, they acquired another dimension. They turned into something else, into a cloud. Besides, the voices, the music, the noise from the motorbikes, rather than rupturing this sense of other-worldliness, intensified it. Because the hubbub reaching your ears from the street below was more like a distant echo of life, completely alien from its visual representation, additional proof that you were in an unreachable place, remote from the other world, remote from the real world.

I slowly realised what captivated the hotel's few regular guests. It can't have been the luxury (although there was certainly something luxurious about it as I said earlier). Finding a luxury hotel is not difficult — some people even enjoy the vulgarity of overwhelming luxury, but I doubt that many become dedicated *habitués*.

This tiny hotel was not even listed in the phone book. Not even its immediate neighbours had heard of it. It was a place for those in the know. A select few. Its guests felt privileged when they compared themselves to others who paid astronomical rates, perhaps five times as much, to stay in faceless, *nouveau riche*, oversized hotels, crammed in between noisy thoroughfares. The Aino's guests did not perhaps have the chance to parade in front of a gargantuan buffet with a dazzling choice of breakfasts, while they could, if they wished, enjoy freshly-baked bread with the fragrant honey Filippos Argyriadis acquired especially every summer from his native island. In short, a place for the discerning.

During my stay there, I did come across some of the regulars. They obviously knew each other well. At first they looked upon me with curiosity, and then began to extract information about me from the reception desk. I can't imagine what Stelios and his father told them. It seemed that they too had their own little *Phi Beta Kappa* going.

My room, Number 8, was a corner room. One side looked onto the main road, above the shops, the other onto the small street where the entrance to the hotel was. There was a small balcony on the first side, a window on the latter. No view from either. Just leaves and branches. Stepping out onto the balcony meant walking into a huge pine tree. It was the only corner room in the hotel – the others all looked onto the main road. Perhaps that was what made it seem privileged.

I was curious to know who else had slept in my bed, who else had mulled over Simos Skouris's ridiculous questions before going to sleep, who else had looked into Argyriadis's penetrating gaze in their attempt to determine the raw materials used in the making of these people. I wondered whether Room 8 was always assigned to probationary candidates.

I asked Stelios.

'No, it doesn't work like that. Mr Argyriadis's last guest was a pianist. She spent a week here. Stayed in 6. The year before last there was somebody else, a mathematician. He was in 5. It always depends on availability. In 8, there's only ever been you and...' He paused. 'I forget his name.'

Without another word, he abandoned the desk and disappeared into the room off the lobby he shared with his father.

There's something else I'll never forgot about the Aino: that pervasive smell, like damp wood imbued with the subtlest aroma of honey – if indeed it is possible to capture a smell in words. I came across it again later; it was very similar if not identical. I was living in Italy by then. One year I was invited to somebody's country house for Easter. I didn't know my hosts and they must have thought I was mad. Every now and then I would inhale large gulps of air through my nostrils like a hunting dog, always with the same verdict; that Aino smell. I couldn't work out what the two places could have in common, beyond the obvious fact that both places were full of old furniture.

Towards the end of the day, I realised that there was more to it: my host was called Filippos; like Argyriadis. But I wondered how these two factors could explain the smell; quite simply they couldn't.

ten

This first episode of sleepwalking was quickly followed by another, possibly even the next evening. I can't remember what led up to it, but it did feature the wardrobe again, only this time with me inside it. I'd opened both doors, pushed the clothes to the sides and sat down on the bottom. I found the whole thing very funny, but it scared me too. What was happening to me? 'There's a wardrobe in my room that calls out to me at night,' I said to myself, half-jokingly; but this throwaway comment took on deeper significance after the episode involving the drawer.

Let me get the sequence of events straight. I'll start with a quick description of the wardrobe. It was a freestanding cupboard, not a built-in wardrobe, an old piece that had once formed part of the Argyriadis collection. Made of light wood, it had a geometrical pattern engraved across the top; the two doors in the mid section were slightly convex and there were four drawers underneath the main hanging space, two small ones on each side. I had filled the entire wardrobe with my neatly arranged belongings.

My underwear was housed in the bottom left-hand drawer. Each time I opened that drawer, I noticed a fine film of brown dust sitting on top of my pristine white vests,

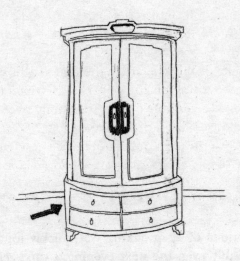

The wardrobe in my room

as though someone had been sprinkling cinnamon all over them. It didn't smell, and all it took was a light blow to get rid of it. At first I found thought it odd, but as time went on, I became profoundly irritated by it. It even occurred to me that someone in the hotel might be practising black magic. I confronted the chambermaid and the cleaner, asking them if they had been opening my drawers. Of course they both hotly denied it. Fortunately, it didn't take long for me to work out what was going on and satisfy myself that nothing was amiss. Each time I opened and shut the drawer above (something I did frequently because I used that drawer for everyday things) the sides scraped against the body of the wardrobe, filing down the wood and depositing the debris inside the drawer beneath, as though someone had been working on it with sandpaper – the powder was that fine. As soon as I realised this, I pulled out the drawer, emptied it, inverted it and gave it a good bashing outside on the balcony, catching the remaining particles of dust with a damp cloth. Afterwards I applied soap to the sides to stop the wood being eaten away.

In the middle of this operation, the drawer still inverted, I noticed some writing on the underside. I wiped the area carefully to reveal a vertical column containing twelve dates. Twelve consecutive November days: the 8th, 9th, 10th and so on until the 19th November. No mention of the year. Each date had the name of one of the group members written next to it – or at least an abbreviated form: Chrys., Arg., Par., Halk., either alternating or running in twos and threes. Skouris's name was nowhere to be seen; perhaps this was before his time. I immediately recognised this list as a schedule of meetings of some other probationary guest, maybe the one whose name Stelios couldn't remember, who had stayed in Room 8. (I did exactly the same thing – I wrote down the date and next to it the name of the member I had seen that day.)

I remembered something Argyriadis had said to me. When you discover something, however inconsequential, you experience the thrill of bringing something hitherto hidden to light: the joy of pulling back the veil, he'd called it. He was right. I suddenly had the urge to go down onto the street holding the drawer aloft and shouting about my discovery for all to hear. I re-examined those crude markings, which looked like the work of a bird pecking and scratching the wooden surface. The four last dates, the 16th, 17th, 18th and 19th of November were blank. The day before, the 15th, had the word 'everybody' next to it, in block capitals. I decided that this person must have written down all the dates as soon as he arrived, filling in the meetings as they went along. The abrupt way the names stopped made me suspect that either they had decided that the entire process was a waste of time, or – and this seemed more likely – this guest had left the Aino early, after only eight of the twelve projected days, straight after the group meeting on the 15th.

Underneath this rudimentary table was a name written in a bizarre hand, more of a logo than an autograph. Ilias Alvertos. The name Stelios couldn't remember. It looked something like this:

Nothing else.

What makes a man write on the underside of a drawer? His way of leaving a mark? Or maybe he'd run out of paper. Whatever the case, he certainly wasn't trying to send a coded message in the hope that one day it would be found. But then again, it had been found, a long time later, found by someone who understood it and was deeply thrilled by it, as though through this discovery he was coming closer to this mystery person.

I went down to reception. Stelios had his head buried in a comic, an adult comic, I suspect.

'Ilias Alvertos,' I said, loud and clear.

He looked up, speechless.

'What are you gawping at? Isn't that the name of the person who stayed in my room?'

His stare was vacant, frozen and dark.

'How do you know that?'

'I know how to sniff things out,' I answered, winking at him, and, just to maintain the suspense, disappeared before he could say another word.

I went back to my room, laughing. I flopped down onto the bed and then looked at the wardrobe once again. With my usual habit of looking to metaphysics for an explanation for everything, I speculated that my recent sleepwalking episodes, just like the appearance of the brown dust, served only one purpose – to direct my attention to that particular piece of furniture. And all that writing underneath the drawer.

eLeven

I inspected the other drawers too but came up with nothing, nothing at all. I briefly flirted with the idea of immortalising my own interview timetable in the same way Ilias Alvertos had, but decided it was too unoriginal. Years later, at another hotel, in another town, I did leave my mark, on the back of a painting, fully conscious that my action bore the stamp of inauthenticity.

Back then, when I was younger, I was constantly at odds with myself; if I admired something about someone, a movement, a grimace, the way they presented their ideas, I would have to check myself, stop myself from trying to adopt that particular feature. I knew that if I did, somewhere, somehow, there would be a watchful eye, monitoring my movements, and the ensuing scorn would automatically neutralise any pleasure to be had from improving myself. Eventually, I managed to give that eye the slip; growing older, I realised that there is an art to assimilating what is admirable in other people.

Let me get back to the events themselves – though I doubt they would stretch to more than three sides, and besides, there is no real danger of their being forgotten, so why the urgency? It's everything else, the elusive moments in between, the unseen side of life at the Aino, the furtive thoughts of its guests, all that could easily recede from memory and must be salvaged at all costs before it's too late.

The day I made that discovery under the drawer I was due to meet Halkiolakis, but when I went downstairs to meet him in the seating area – I had received instructions to meet him there the night before – I saw the photographer there in his place.

'Our director had to leave,' she explained. 'You're stuck with me today, I'm afraid. If you don't mind, that is.'

Why would I mind? I was under contract to make myself available to the group and it made no difference to me whom I spent the time with.

'I thought we might go somewhere, get away from base a little.'

I was happy to. We got into her small car. She didn't tell me where we were headed. She wanted it to be a surprise. Tina Paraschis was always very relaxed and warm with me, but this time, although she was by no means cold, I did detect a subtle change in her behaviour. I couldn't put my finger on it, but something was definitely on her mind. I can't remember what we talked about in the car, only that I did ask her where her name came from. She told me that 'Tina' was short for 'Argentina': Spanish grandmother.

We were driving towards the sea and before long were caught up in rush hour port traffic. Immobilised, all we could see for miles around were other vehicles that had come to a standstill. Then we headed west and emerging from the docks, I could see what her surprise was; she was going to take me for a trip on an out-of-commission ship. I was stunned.

These people certainly knew how to leave you dumbfounded. True, there was something pretentious about them, and their desire to set themselves apart from the *hoi polloi* frequently made them come across as arrogant and eccentric, even ridiculous. But you had to hand it to them; they had a talent for discovering beauty where the ordinary eye would never care to hover, and a way of suddenly spiriting you off to uncharted territory. When I sit down and think about it, I have to admit that I owe them a lot, and despite all the unpleasantness that followed, I will always acknowledge the fact that they left an indelible stamp on the way I see things, the way I see everything.

She pointed out the ship to me from the car and I wondered how we were going to get down there. A short distance from the harbour was a string of cafeterias and bars. We stopped the car and went into one of them; I stood by the door while she strode through the bar and stopped to talk to a man sitting on his own at the back. As soon as he saw her, he got up. They exchanged a few words and made their way back to me.

'This is Nikos. He's taking us out to the ship.'

The three of us set off on foot until we reached a small promontory. We boarded the motorboat belonging to this Nikos character, and made out to sea. The weather was sultry, the water a listless grey.

The noise from the engine, in combination with Nikos's presence, encouraged Paraschis to open up to me about what was on her mind, what had made her seem a little remote that day. Sometimes it's easier to talk about sensitive matters when there's a huge racket in the background than it is during moments of complete silence.

'Who told you about Ilias?'

I knew exactly what she meant, but I have no idea why I chose to pretend I didn't.

'Ilias who?'

'Ilias Alvertos.'

I laughed. She looked relieved. I told her the whole story

about the drawer, making light of it, and reassuring her that that was the extent of my knowledge about Ilias Alvertos. Her entire demeanour changed. She turned her face to the wind, which promptly cleared her face of her hair, and stretched out calmly to look at the waves. I, on the other hand, instead of relaxing, had started to wonder.

For the first time I suspected that the last-minute alteration to the programme was no chance event. The fact that I had mentioned the name of Ilias Alvertos seemed to have hit a nerve in the group, and they had obviously thought it best for Paraschis to confront me, probably because she knew me slightly better than the others. Her brief – I concluded – was to find out what I knew and what I did not know about Alvertos. At least that's what my instincts told me, and the more I thought about it, the more various speculations started working their way through my head, the gentle creaking sound of the boat the natural accompaniment to this process.

I considered the last blank entries in his diary, which suggested that he had left the Aino early, after the last group meeting. I was almost convinced that something horrible had happened, something so bad that he had packed up and left. I was sure that if I managed to find out what that was, my view of the group would change at once. So this was what all this fuss was about; I had suspected as much. I also recalled Stelios's frosty reaction when I mentioned Alvertos's name. Everything was coming together.

We were getting close. There was a strange, salty wetness between my teeth, an irritating crunchiness. I saw a ladder being lowered down the side of the ship; somebody wearing a cap was waiting for us at the top. Nikos did everything he could to bring his boat flush with the ship, but the nearer he got, the point at which my foot would have to leave the uncertain surface of his boat for the slippery steel of the ladder filled me, at any rate, with unease, if not sheer dread. But the photographer was made of sterner stuff, and successfully pulled off the jump with a deft twirl. She started the ascent to the deck, totally unconcerned about my fate while I remained irresolute on the boat. A sudden wave compounded the pressure I felt from Nikos, who shot me the impatient glare of one delayed.

'If you don't watch your step, you could end up in the water,' I said feebly, hoping for some advice.

'That's right,' he replied in a tone far from reassuring.

I broke out in a cold sweat. I didn't know how to swim. I can't swim. Looking him straight in the eye, I asked myself whether he would jump in after me if something did go wrong. I thought not.

Meanwhile, Paraschis had reached the top of the ladder where the man with the cap was waiting. They both stood there, looking down at me, waiting for my next move in silence. Six eyes upon me.

Eventually the rocking motion of the boat evened out. The sea was calm but the boatman impatient.

'Go on! What are you afraid of? Jump!'

A diabolical face: covered in spots; beady little eyes, set too close together; sticking-out ears – that was Nikos.

The distance seemed small. I raised my right leg with very little difficulty, all it took was a little push, and I had to take advantage of the moment and jump while the wind was still holding its breath.

I didn't make it. Unhappily. The fact that I escaped getting completely submerged in water is something, I suppose, because if I had fallen in, that would have been it. My leap was pathetic; I mean, my right leg could have made it safely onto the ladder, but my left was too slow to follow. Fear might have been responsible for that. My foot simply didn't get there in time and my leg was completely drenched up to the calf. I heard (or possibly imagined), a chuckle coming from the direction of the boat. I didn't feel humiliated about slipping; the joy of being alive and safe overwhelmed any such feeling, even though the mocking sound of water swilling around my toes inside my shoe was clearly audible throughout my ascent up the ladder.

I made it to the top and stepped on deck, a huge, metallic plateau.

'This is Pavlos. He guards the ship. He's the...'

'Get wet, did you?' he asked.

'Oh, it's nothing,' I said, pleased that the gurgling sound inside my shoe was getting fainter all the time.

With that we began our tour of the floating metal. Paraschis seemed to be on familiar territory. She told me that she had been to the ship twice before, to photograph it for a magazine article on out-of-commission ships.

One Saturday, several years ago, while I was still at school, we went to the cinema. When I got home I noticed that one of the small silver chains I used to wear round my wrist was missing. Armed with a torch, I retraced my steps but there was no sign of it. The cinema had closed by the time I got there, so I went back the next day when I knew the cleaner would be there. The door was open. The silence, the emptiness, the daylight flooding in through the emergency exit, those three things transformed that familiar place into something strange, something unnatural, something else.

That was pretty much how I felt that day on the ship. Summer images were still alive in my mind: hordes of tourists with their colourful luggage scattered all over the deck, the endless queues at the bar for coffee, and the irrepressible hubbub, compared with the wasteland I was now confronted with, disconcerted me and the entire scene struck me as belonging to another dimension. I did have my share of experience of deserted houses which I loved exploring as a child, but at least there everything would be covered in dust, a film of grit which penetrated every gap and crack, gradually hardening on the walls, floors and the relics of furniture. There was no dust here, just a pervasive, saline grime, with the same colonizing tendencies as house dust. You could see it, and smell it, and feel it under the soles of your feet.

We walked up steps, we walked down steps, we walked down corridors, we walked up corridors, we went inside cabins, we looked through port holes – all the images from the ship surface in my mind in a jumble; I can't remember the order we saw anything in or where we saw it. We opened doors, closed doors, door after door; I remember seeing some clothes strewn about somewhere: shirts and trousers, and in one metal cupboard we found piles of papers, various shipping documents and the like, as well as somebody's wedding photo, not the youngest couple I'd ever seen, but they looked happy.

But there's another image that has remained equally vivid. Somewhere there was a narrow wooden table with three glasses standing on it, and three chairs nesting around it. Who knows who'd sat on those chairs, what they'd said, what they'd had to drink. Just for a bit of fun, the three of us sat down, lifted the glasses and clinked them together in a toast. The photographer switched on the square torch she had in her bag; it was an unusual design, something like a lantern that shone from every side. We each began to indulge in our own versions of armchair philosophy, and I could picture my own face, dimly lit, grave and unsmiling.

The conversation soon turned to the past, the past in general and then to our personal pasts. In a lighter mood, relieved of her earlier concerns, she relaxed and began to share tales from her youth with us. That was when she told me about their theatre group, how their friendship sprung up, and how they initiated themselves into the world of the arts.

All four of them – Simos Skouris, as I've already told you, was a later addition – broke away almost immediately from the other actors, as though in response to the common fate that would bind them. This was especially true of Filippos Argyriadis and Petros Halkiolakis; they became inseparable. Whenever one of them turned up, you could be sure the other wasn't far behind. Their relationship was open to misinterpretation, but the photographer said that she was prepared to put her hand in fire and swear that there was nothing more than a deep friendship that bound them. Unfortunately, Argyriadis *père* did not share this confidence. Widely considered to be harsh and unscrupulous (as Paraschis put it), he asked his son to put an end to his association with the theatre crowd, and in particular that suspect young man. Seeing his words had fallen on deaf ears and hearing tongues wagging more and more audibly, he changed tactics. He summoned Petros Halkiolakis, snarling his ultimatum, 'Keep away from my son or there'll be consequences.' Halkiolakis was quite unmoved, but shortly afterwards met with an accident. He was knocked over by a motorcycle in a hit and run. He was saved by a miracle, but the message was unambiguous: Argyriadis was deadly serious.

But so was Halkiolakis. A few days later, there was another accident. It bore the marks of the first one, involving another reckless motorcyclist. The only difference was that this time it was old Argyriadis who was left for dead. He was rushed to hospital, underwent a series of operations, but never recovered the full use of his legs. He went around with a crutch until the day he died. The group, Filippos Argyriadis included, followed these events in silence, in stunned passivity, without comment, not even among themselves. It was years before they could bring themselves to talk about it and of course not before the old man died.

Everybody expected that after the director's response to the old man (nobody ever doubted that he was behind the second accident) old Argyriadis would have been even more determined to be rid of the brazen young man. But he just kept himself to himself, and never involved himself in the matter again. He stopped telling his son what company he should keep. Either he had been given the fright of his life or he had been forced to acknowledge and submit to the superior strength of his opponent. I asked the photographer about him:

'Is it true that he was mixed up with the Junta, and before that with the Nazis?'

'Where did you get that from? Another drawer?' she chuckled.

(Ah! I've just remembered something. Of course. That's it! The workings of the memory are so opaque. The entire scene with the narrow table, the three chairs, the three glasses, the revelations about the old man's past and the Halkiolakis story, all of the preceding conversation – none of that took place on the ship. Of course it didn't. No. We'd disembarked by then, and were making our way back to the car. It had started to rain, and there, on the road, was a bus shelter, whitewashed, like a small cubicle and we dashed under it to keep dry. The table with the chairs and the glasses was in there. We clinked glasses in fun. It's strange; I can remember every last, insignificant detail, down to the dirt smudges left on my hand by the glass, but I had managed to forget where it had all happened. But now I am certain. It was in the bus shelter.)

twelve

It is the twelfth day, in line with the number at the top of the page, the twelfth day of sitting here writing about everything that happened back then. I don't mean it's the twelfth consecutive day. There's usually a break of sorts in between, a couple of days, before I go back to my notebook. If, for argument's sake, I wrote the story of the ship on a Wednesday, then it follows that today is Sunday. Each time I go back to it, I move on numerically, doing things in sections: that way I'll know how long the whole thing has taken me. If I need to break off and continue later in the day, it won't count as a new section. But if I stop for the day, the next time I sit down and write, I'll leave three lines at the end of the last section blank and start a new one. Not that it matters much, but it does help me round off my thoughts for the day within a single section. I don't always succeed. I worry that if I lose concentration and leave something half-finished, I will have completely lost the thread by the time I get back to it; as if things weren't complicated enough already.

Shortly after the Aino disaster, I left for Italy to do a post-graduate degree, working on digs, hoping to get a job at the university. Not long into my stay there, a friend of mine, a law student, filled me in on the latest developments in the group.

After that, I lost interest and became increasingly involved in my new environment and tried to put all that behind me. I haven't given them much thought over the last few years, and beyond the occasional unexpected, involuntary flashbacks, they have remained buried safely, like Pompeii, under the lava. Now that I'm back, I've resolved to salvage these memories piece by piece, and work on them with a wire brush. I look on in astonishment as they leap up before me, large as life, while all this time I had believed they lay foundering in the depths. I pick up my pencil and start writing: I summon them, they hear and they respond. Reconstruction begins.

Solid phrases come to mind, fragments of conversations, and I enlist the help of my imagination to reconstitute the rest. My imagination does play a role, but not an arbitrary one. After all, it wouldn't be natural if I could still recall these conversations verbatim, or remember how the protagonists of a particular scene progressed from one thought to another. However much we like to insist that we can remember every last detail of a picture from the past, there are always aspects that elude us. We might say, for example, 'I can remember that day we visited our aunt at her place in the country and we found her in the kitchen preparing greens; it's as though I can see her standing in front of me.' But if we ask ourselves what she was wearing, the colour of her apron, her slippers, we'll have to admit the impossibility of recalling all those details, which only a photograph has the capacity to preserve, not the memory. However, when we picture auntie, she is invariably fully clad, not naked, but what have we dressed her in, bearing in mind that we can't remember what she was actually wearing? It is only when we pose the problem with hindsight that we focus on this detail of our mental picture. If we picture her in a brown cardigan or green dressing gown that she might have worn on some other occasion, it is not because she was wearing those garments on that day. She may never have owned them at all, and only acquired them through our mentally outfitting her with a suitable wardrobe.

This is exactly how I fill in the gaps in my memory of all the scenes I describe, and I think I can legitimately write that Filippos Argyriadis turned and looked at me searchingly at such and such a point; it may have been just before or just after he shot me that look – it might not have been a look at all, it could just as easily have been a few words. The point is that Filippos Argyriadis had communicated surprise and it is my job to relate that fact. It's true that sometimes I am given to exaggeration. I don't feel the slightest bit guilty about that either; I am not trying to distort the truth, just trying to set it in relief. All the better to remember it.

Trying to establish the correct sequence of events always gives me a headache. I can never get it straight, whether something happened before or after something else, or whether something happened on the third, fifth or the twelfth day. Not always, of course. Some events are landmark events, and their position in the sequence is never in question. I try to work out the order of occurrences, and with the help of associations, try to impose order on my confused material. And that can be difficult.

Then again, there are times when I think that it is precisely this mist, this mould, which to an extent has enveloped both people and events, which, however contradictory it may sound, can actually help me to a deeper understanding. Standing too close, in too intense a light, can do more to distort than clarify your vision. And the scattered pieces, the dismembered and the unconnected, highlight the details more precisely than the whole.

Whatever. Some things have been forgotten. Lost and forgotten. Other things would have been difficult to put into words, which is understandable, and only to be expected. I'll try to do this at least: put everything that has survived in my memory down on paper, using signs to guide my thoughts like slogans ('open sesame!') and awaken in me everything that lies hidden and cannot be captured within the lines of this notebook.

Paraschis told me some more things about Argyriadis *père*. But that will have to wait for tomorrow and a clear head.

thirteen

The first thing she did was confirm what I'd been told about Argyriadis's collaboration with the Germans. She also told me a story from those days.

One evening, possibly towards the end of the Occupation, old Argyriadis (not so old back then) was walking towards the Aino (not the Aino back then but the Phoenix). The Germans had requisitioned the entire building, and had even stationed some kind of command in there so access was restricted. Argyriadis was a regular visitor; rumour had it that he played cards with the officers of an evening. That evening, as he was walking through a small coppice (where the shopping centre is today, she explained) on his way to the hotel, in the red light of dusk, he made out the silhouette of a woman sitting in a pine tree. She was trying to get at something with a stick, like you would if you were trying to dislodge a piece of fruit, an odd thing to be doing up a pine tree. When she finally managed to get a grip on what turned out to be a small nest, she climbed down the tree. She removed the eggs one by one, pierced their shells with a fine needle, top and bottom, and sucked.

Argyriadis, when greeted with this sight, considered approaching the hungry waif and offering her a job as a chambermaid at the hotel, working for the Germans, of course. He knew they were looking for someone. The woman couldn't talk, she was a mute, but not deaf – a combination Argyriadis thought ideal in the circumstances. She was also utterly lacking in initiative. Perfect.

She started work immediately. Apart from a sister, she was alone in the world, and did not need to explain herself to anyone. She settled into the lumber-room, the same place where I was to stumble across Filippos Argyriadis many years later. It was hard work. She was required to do everything: mop, clean, iron and keep boots polished. She didn't have to cook as they had their own person for that. She was on her feet constantly from dawn till nightfall, but was never disgruntled, never showed signs of being tired. On the contrary, she was very happy and viewed the arrangement as fair: her labour in exchange for board and lodging, and as much food as she wanted. She had never eaten so much or so well in her life, and was also able to keep her sister and her family fed most of the time.

(Her sister could still be alive today. She was eight years ago, when I appeared at the Aino. I saw her myself once through the window, on her way in to visit Argyriadis. It wasn't till my conversation with Paraschis that I realised who she was.)

So, everyone was happy. The starving woman was fattened up and she never once imagined that her behaviour might come across to the outside world as leaving something to be desired. You could see that her capacity to tell right from wrong was impaired, as were her emotions. After all, she didn't lose her father, a brother, or husband in that war; if she had, it might have given her a jolt. The only feelings she could muster for those uniformed men who she was ordered to obey, were awe and respect. She didn't even take offence when they breezed through her room at night on their way up to the terrace for guard duty, let their hands roam all over her fleshy beauty. She never seemed put out when some of them threw her to the ground and had their way with her; it had the opposite effect. She experienced the fact that these stern (and therefore important) men noticed her existence, unambiguously as a blessing. A personal blessing.

Argyriadis proved a regular blessing himself after a hand or two of cards. She would wait for him eagerly, in anticipation of the delicious treats he would produce afterwards, things that were hard to get hold of, even inside the paradise of plenty she inhabited. Spicy salami, juicy sweets wrapped in crinkly paper.

When challenged by her sister, she insisted with outraged gestures that there was no abuse. Her sister had got wind of what was going on and rushed over to knock some sense into her. It never once occurred to the chambermaid that she was being treated badly, that she was a victim. Why would it? She was contented and had absolutely no intention of leaving despite her sister's attempts to persuade her to, both by pleading with her and trying to frighten her. Where would she go? She was about to accuse her sister of being jealous of her privileged position, and was not going to do her the favour of leaving her protectors, certainly not now that she was pregnant.

'Eating for two now.' There was no moving her. Nothing was said about the father of her baby, of course. It could have been any of a number of candidates, but they weren't exactly lining up to claim paternity.

The defeat of the Germans and their retreat a few months later signalled the end of her happiness. She was on the verge of giving birth. I could picture her, tearful, clutching her huge, swollen stomach and bidding farewell, one by one, to her protectors. She was alone in the empty hotel but Argyriadis didn't throw her onto the street. Perhaps he suspected that he could have been the father, even though he knew full well that there had been several forks partaking of the same dish.

Her sister came back, this time with another relative, a midwife. They both moved in to the hotel with their families to look after her until the baby was born.

Labour took place in the lumber-room. With the assistance of the midwife, everything went smoothly. The relatives left, mother and baby stayed on. A couple of years later, she died of a heart attack, perhaps overeating contributed. Argyriadis adopted the child with the help of a notary public, and from that day on, nobody ever questioned little Filippos's paternity.

fourteen

I'd swear on my mother's grave that Filippos Argyriadis was not his father's son. There's no way on this earth. The man's features were obviously Germanic; I had noticed that before I heard the stories from the war. It was the first thing that struck me about him, that he looked foreign. German, maybe Swedish, but definitely not home grown.

There was a photograph up in the lumber-room inside an art deco frame, standing on his desk. It was of a woman, with chubby cheeks, wavy hair falling across her forehead and a wide collar. I assumed it was his mother. Next to it, in a smaller, square frame, stood a picture of a man wearing round spectacles with sunken cheeks. Agyriadis *père*. If there had been any resemblance to the mother, you might think that the son had inherited something from her side, but the collector emphatically did not take after either parent, but was the spitting image of the German; the fact there was no photograph of said German on the desk was a minor detail.

I don't believe that the thought that he was illegitimate bothered him unduly. He may even have been grateful for escaping old Argyriadis's genes. I have no idea whether he found out about it as a boy or was much older, or whether it was his father, or some aunt who had taken him aside to reveal the truth. Judging by the way Paraschis told me the story, I gathered that the subject was neither taboo or in anyway sensitive within the group, or confidential.

I had already realised that the collector was not the sort of person to accord importance to things other people found mortifying, or the sort of person who would ever go to the trouble of concealing them. Not that sort of thing anyway.

fifteen

The days at the Aino passed, the Earth continued to turn on its axis with the same prehistoric rhythms, while my five satellite planets continued to circle around me. Time was moving fast and I tried to understand what was going on, how this extraordinary experiment was shaping up, whether they were getting anything out of all this, out of me, or whether, when all was said and done, they were satisfied with their decision to invite me.

I must admit that at first I was prepared for a much more rigorous trial – precisely what I thought that involved I can't say, perhaps that they intended to use me as a guinea pig and put me through all kinds of ordeals. In the event, things were much calmer, they were very friendly towards me, and although I did occasionally smell danger in the air, that probably had more to do with my own suspicious mind than anything else.

Nevertheless, I didn't see how they could possibly benefit from observing me, from watching someone with less than half their knowledge, someone totally devoid of any kind of special gift or rare talent. In my opinion they were wasting their money, and I felt bad about it, but there was not a great deal I could do about it. I paraded my unsmiling face about the place, and made sure that at least I was punctual for all my meetings.

From a practical point of view, the only one of the five who tried to take advantage of my presence was the director. He would read me passages from the script of a film he was planning to make, and would then ask me to put myself in the shoes of the various characters and tell him how I thought they would react. I was happy to oblige; it was like a game, but as far as I know, the film was never made, and I don't remember that much about it.

I was afraid of him, especially after hearing everything the photographer told me – and how casually she did so! – about his stand-off with Argyriadis *père*. He was the only one who had this effect on me. I was in no doubt that he could be quite ruthless if necessary. His image was deceptive; he had a cheerful and appealing face, and that, in combination with his generous, bulky frame, reminded me more of an upright bear, a strong, dangerous animal, which, no matter how familiar you are with it, you can never quite let go of the fear that it might suddenly lash out at you. One day, while we were sitting quietly working away on the script, he suddenly leapt to his feet, walked over to me and grabbed hold of my knee, squeezed it with his fist and started groping it. And then he let go, gathered up the script, and returned to the text. It was only after quite some time had passed, that he actually commented on this action.

'You can learn a lot about people from their knees, yours are square, which means that you think a great deal, you make use of your brain. Most intellectuals are square-kneed.'

If that is the case, this was the first I'd heard of it. And the last. But ever since then, I have made a point of inspecting people's knees. If I spot a rounded one, I automatically write the owner off as brainless. Of course I don't believe a word of it, but it did affect me somehow.

The good thing was that they all spoke completely openly about each other in front of me, even making barbed comments, without the slightest hesitation; it was as though they were looking to me for support. Of course, they would never have gone ahead with any conversation or revelation that would have put anyone in a difficult position, never in front of an outside party, but there was a constant, free flow of barbed comments. I remember when I asked Halkiolakis if he had ever collaborated with Chryssovergis professionally. It seemed like an obvious thing to wonder about a director and an actress who happened to be friends. His answer:

'Unfortunately our actress is not cut out for film. She's only any good in the theatre. What's more, she's not in the least photogenic. Looks dreadful.'

The next day, feigning ignorance, I asked Chryssovergis the same question. She said:

'No way! I could never put up with his hysterical outbursts. He'll be all calm one minute and then suddenly start screaming at the top of his lungs. God, he's a regular *prima donna*. I'd be out of there like a shot. It drives me mad every time he tells me that I'd be perfect for such and such a part and later discover that he's got some hideously ugly female part in mind.'

Now that we are on the subject of the actress, I have to admit that she was not nearly as arrogant during our subsequent meetings as she had been the first time we met. What I mean is that she was less condescending towards me, even though she still made a show of being the great intellectual, in a way that reminded me a lot of Filippos Argyriadis. There was certainly a difference, a considerable difference. For the collector, sitting around dispensing wisdom was second nature to him, a function of his spirit, a mirror image of the workings of his mind, whereas for the actress it was more like a fashion accessory. Not that she talked rubbish; she didn't. I can still remember some of the things she said which were quite impressive. It was just that you always had the feeling that it was all second hand, or borrowed from The Great Book of whatever the subject under discussion happened to be.

'Great artists should never be regarded as such by other people. They are nothing more than the vehicle through which Art chooses to manifest itself. Talent is nothing more than the dependence that Art itself bestows on the artists in order to serve it. Artists are ministers, not God; they are the mirror, not the image.'

One of her set pieces. I liked it and made a note of it on the back flyleaf of a book, and recently copied it from there, eight years later.

I have said this before, and I will say it again: I observed them just as closely and just as carefully as they observed me. Of course, they had no idea this was the case. The only difference was that I was not paying them, they were paying me. I studied them, I analysed them, and now that I have a better understanding of them, I am putting it all down in writing.

We were into the second week of my stay (it's funny, but I didn't really experience the time I spent there by the week, but in five-day phases, three five-day chunks). When the programme for the following day was slipped under my door late one evening, I saw that a group meeting had been timetabled for the first time. It filled me with panic – our first group meeting at the hotel.

It wasn't the thought of coming face to face with all five of them at once. By then I was used to them, and besides, during the trial period right at the beginning of our acquaintance, there had been group meetings. What unsettled me was what I had read underneath that drawer, which made me suspect that it was after a similar group meeting that Ilias Alvertos had decided to take off from the Aino.

We met in the small lounge at six on the dot. It was a beautiful evening and when somebody suggested that we transfer to the roof terrace, everyone immediately agreed, nobody more than I, who felt a certain relief at the prospect of a meeting in an open space. Stelios brought up some white folding director's chairs and the whole place suddenly resembled a film set. The roof was completely bare, there wasn't even a television aerial or a solar heating tank up there. Completely bare with the exception of a metal weather vane with the silhouette of a cockerel sitting on top of it. This cockerel, apart from informing you of the direction of the wind, was obliging enough to point out the four points on the horizon. The terrace was marked off by a low wall instead of the usual railings, too low to reassure those afflicted with vertigo. The floor was covered in stone slabs, heavily eroded by weather and scorching sun. The trees encircling the building provided a natural parapet, obscuring the beautiful view which suddenly, magically, greeted you each time the wind blew an opening between them.

Weather vane with cockerel silhouette

It was Spring. April. The evening sun was most welcome. The bars and restaurants below were still closed so it was relatively quiet too. The chairs were scattered around, not particularly close together. We sat down. Small talk and glasses of orange juice changed hands; a party atmosphere. I could see Filippos Argyriadis approaching me. This was the first time I'd seen him since that night. In an ambivalent voice he said:

'I thought that we might meet tomorrow. I have hardly seen you at all, and am looking forward to having that little chat about Aino. Remember?'

Not what I wanted to hear.

'What time?' was all I could manage to say through my anxiety. As if the time mattered.

'Ten tomorrow morning. I'll be waiting there,' he said, pointing to his room.

'I am not convinced that there is anything I can say that you don't already know,' I said, lamely. 'Little is known on the subject and I remember even less.'

'No matter. Your knowledge, however minimal, may be of great value to me. I'll be expecting you.' He walked off.

I put off thinking about it. I would have an entire night for that. I focused my attention on the here and now instead. Chryssovergis, from the other end of the terrace, raised her glass and made a toast:

'To the health of our most inscrutable guest ever!'

'Hear, hear!' applauded Halkiolakis. 'We've never been so divided in our opinion of anyone. This tells us something: he's no open book.'

'There's no division – just a difference of opinion. Personally, with every meeting, I am forced to revise the conclusions I made the previous time, and I think it's worth pointing out that I have seen more of him than the rest of you.'

This was Simos Skouris, jumping at the chance to show how diligent and dutiful he had been.

It had never occurred to me that I was in the least inscrutable. Reserved and cautious, yes. I realised then that apart from the meetings that they had had with me, they had been getting together and sharing thoughts. And not only that; they had been speculating about me, testing their hypotheses in the meetings I attended. When, for example, the director asked me how old I was when I lost my virginity, he might have wanted to see if he had guessed right, nothing else. They were making bets about me, setting traps, and were lying in wait to see if I would fall into them or jump over them. As soon as I realised this, I understood that there was another aspect to this process which I had not suspected, the game aspect. An unpredictable game in which the basic piece is a living, autonomous entity. My curiosity was partly indulged by this: what was it about me that had them so fascinated? If indeed I was inscrutable, all the better for the game!

'So how can we find out more about you?' asked Paraschis, laughing.

'I always answer your questions. I am always at your disposal. What is that you want to know?'

My good-natured response proved disarming. This did not escape the director.

'Nobody has any complaints there. The trouble is your answers. Instead of exposing you, they obscure you. You never reveal yourself.'

'How do you get a man in waterproofs wet?' This from the scholarly Simos Skouris.

'What do you expect him to do?' The photographer was about to come to my defence. 'After all, doesn't the beauty of all this reside in the mystery?'

The collector, who had so far refrained from contributing

to the discussion, began to speak very quietly. The others immediately stopped talking in order to listen. At first his voice was no more than a faint breath.

'...some people you never manage to get to know in depth. Either because they won't let you, and they keep you at a distance, or because there is no depth to them. It's as simple as that. In the case of our friend, it is quite obvious which category he belongs to. On that point at least, we are all agreed.' He had his back turned to me, and was talking about me as though I were absent. 'Let's deal with the other matter. What are we going to do? I am wondering, as I am sure you are too: is he determined to stay put in his fortress until the end, or has he perhaps not found a way to venture forth from there. Both intriguing eventualities. It shouldn't be too difficult to predict which of the two will prove to be the case, luckily. We will show him the way to open up. If he accepts the challenge, it means he's not as impregnable as we believed. If he refuses, well, we'll see...'

They obviously knew what he meant and acknowledged it in half-smiles. And for not entirely obscure reasons, I couldn't get the image of Ilias Alvertos out of my mind. The Ilias Alvertos I had fashioned in my imagination.

sixteen

Back at my desk.

They pulled their chairs in, forming a half circle around me. The relaxed atmosphere had gone; everybody was on the alert. Filippos Argyriadis eventually turned to face me.

'Danger is by definition a bad thing. People want to avoid danger. They don't like insecurity and fear. It's bad for them. But, if you know that in the final analysis, nothing bad is going to happen to you, danger can be such a sweet sensation. If you know that its hands are tied, you can face up to it, scrutinise it, feel its breath on your cheek. Just think about all those people who get a rush from bunjee jumping off bridges, or climb into iron cages that are thrown to the sharks: it's the point where danger turns to pleasure, the pleasure of sticking your tongue out at the impotent beast.'

He took a hearty swig of tomato juice.

'Pleasure of this kind, we can offer you ourselves. If, that is, you want it. You are free to turn us down; the decision is yours.'

This sounded like a marketing ploy from one of those companies that want to give you a free trial of their product, no obligations. The collector, who knew all about marketing strategies, was employing the same tactics.

'If you accept, it'll look good on your C.V. And we'll

have the satisfaction of knowing that we were able to break through your protective outer shell. Too much talk is poverty. I'll get to the point.'

A moment of silence.

'You will share with us your most deeply buried, darkest, guarded secret. The one you would never dare reveal to anyone, the one that makes you break out in a cold sweat at the mere thought of anyone discovering it. You'd die of shame and terror. That's all we ask. A secret.'

Secrets again. Now they were asking me to give them a secret, to hand them a valuable part of myself. To trust them, like Faust trusted the Devil. Danger. And the safety net that would catch my fall in this leap into the void, their silence? The absolute, eternal commitment to keep their lips firmly sealed, and keep my secret safely in their collection, a prized possession, inaccessible to the rest of the world.

They were all opposite me. The sun had set. They were assembled all around and were watching me like wolves. A pack of wolves coming out in the twilight. They were waiting for me to speak.

I can't tell whether it was the intensity of those stares or Filippos Argyriadis's seductive voice. And I can't understand, even today, why I took the unconsidered decision to accept their terms. Perhaps it was because I knew that the secret I would share with them would make them absolutely ecstatic (I had a veritable jewel hidden away inside me for any collector). Perhaps it was much simpler than that. Perhaps it was just time to bring it to light, the opportunity I'd been waiting for for so long. Without actually giving them a straight 'yes' or 'no', I launched into my narrative.

Of course I don't intend to reproduce everything I said to them that night, to lay myself bare all over again – even though I know that the notebook is kept safe in a dead place. Experience has taught me that letters and notebooks, however carefully stashed away in drawers and cupboards, have a habit of resurfacing. Just like a ball, however hard you push it under water, sooner or later it will leap back up to the surface. Because I think that it's worth mentioning two things about the scene that followed, I'll discuss the matter in code, and if I'm the only one who understands it, so be it.

I started off explaining how the first shadow fell. I mean the incident in the kitchen and my part in it. The noise made by all the things as they fell to the floor in shock. The way the others reacted. The changes in their behaviour. The lack of trust that remained among us for a long time afterwards. I talked about F's visits to the house and the ramifications these visits had for us all. They asked me how long this went on for and my answer was that it was that they could very well be continuing, even as we spoke. That made a huge impression on them. Skouris even asked if I had any more recent information. I told him I didn't.

I could feel their excitement growing. And I hadn't even got half way through the story. They asked me feverishly if I could give them as much detail as possible about the people involved, describing their features, and the photographer wanted to know if I had any photographs of them on me. Unfortunately I had to disappoint her.

Then I came to the green file. I took them through it at a very slow, almost sadistically slow, pace. I held all the best bits back for later. At first they suspected nothing, I'm sure they didn't, they couldn't imagine how the two things were connected. The incident in the kitchen and the green file. I gave them a clue. I turned to Filippos Argyriadis and looked deep into his eyes, and saw something flicker there. Nobody else was onto me. I went on a little more.

L Street. I described the place exactly, how the man in charge took me and led me inside. What I said. What they said. I didn't hesitate to go into specifics. I wanted to give as full a picture as I could. Once I'd got into my stride, I was determined to tell them everything, no matter how indifferent they may have been to what I was telling them. I didn't care. The moment was important, not just for them but for me too, perhaps more so for me. The game was going to be played by my rules, and if I wanted to mention the ashtray sitting on top of the desk, I would do so without asking anyone's permission. On the other hand, although they were desperate to get to the heart of the matter, they wanted to hear everything, more than everything.

The number 4588. As the story took this turn, I wasn't sure whether I would be able to remember and repeat everything I knew then, everything I'd been told about that four-digit number. Specifics, I mean. Facts about the course of the situation then as well as about future developments. However, it wasn't difficult for me, at all – I could even say that the words rolled off my tongue, the words I'd read, everything I'd seen written under the 4588. It seems that when you learn something in a state of over-stimulation, it gets recorded in indelible ink. I remembered everything and I delivered it in a single breath.

The grey fabric, saliva, the hands. When I reached this point, they had, I think, stopped breathing. It would have been easy for them to make a quick connection and see how everything hung together. But they didn't. They refused to. They didn't want to reach any conclusions independently. They wanted to be spoon-fed by me, for me to lick the plate clean and tell them that 'b' and 'a' make 'ba'.

The floor. I told them. I summoned all the courage I had in me. The floor. My voice was not my own. How else could it have spoken those words? And then I didn't have anything else to say or explain. I had given them everything, I had reached the end.

Skouris took a deep intake of breath. Chryssovergis was

drying her eyes. Halkiolakis turned his back and sealed himself off from the rest. Paraschis lifted her gaze to the sky and Argyriadis didn't take his eyes off me for one second.

It had grown quite dark. I remember it was quite windy. The wind was fanning the swaying branches and I sat and stared at the distant city lights shining between them.

seventeen

I slept soundly at first. It seemed that the effort of getting all this off my chest had exhausted me. A sweet, restorative sleep – recompense for the courage I had shown. No restlessness, no rehashing everything that had happened in my dreams. But it can't have lasted more than two or three hours. I woke up and found myself consumed by anxiety for the coming day when I would have to face Filippos Argyriadis.

I had handled the Aino business very badly. Because of my pride, because I didn't want to seem ignorant, I had succeeded in painting myself into a corner and now the moment of truth had arrived. After my research had turned up absolutely nothing, even Professor Marneris had drawn a blank, all the evidence suggested that there was no such name, so why did I, idiot that I am, have to insist that I knew all about it? Lying has a way of doing that to you. When you tell a lie, it's hard to back down later, and that pushes you further along the dead end of falsehood, until there is no turning back.

I begged for the night to come to an end quickly, so that I could get this over with. I couldn't restrain myself and found myself knocking on his door twenty minutes early. Before I left my room, I took off my watch to erase all signs of impatience. Then I changed my mind and put it back on, putting it ten minutes forward: the watch lost time, I was in a hurry – we'd split the difference.

I lifted the huge hurricane lamp from the armchair and sat down. No mention was made of my admirable performance the night before, and so, without any word of encouragement to boost my morale, we went straight to the business of the day: 'What do you know about Aino?' He was serious, morose even.

'To be quite honest,' I said, without being in the least honest, 'I can't recall much about Aino, as I mentioned to you yesterday. I'm sure that I've heard a great deal about the name, stories and such, but when I try to recollect details, I come up with almost nothing.'

'Yesterday you indicated that you did remember a few things.'

'Yes, a few insignificant points, verging on nothing.'

'An indistinct memory, in other words.'

'Precisely. An indistinct memory.'

'Tell me about it.'

He was not about to let it go. A determined German.

'I remember once during a seminar, there had been some confusion,' since my hands were tied, I told another lie. 'We were discussing a text, and I can vaguely remember it was about Aino, who – if I'm not mistaken – was a warrior woman.'

He burst out laughing.

'Aino the warrior woman! Where did you get such an idea from?'

'Or was she a concubine?'

'Don't make things worse.'

'Like I said, it's only a vague memory.'

'Vague or non-existent? This is pure invention on your part.'

His tone worried me.

'Perhaps her occupation escapes me, but she definitely came up in one of our seminars.'

'You're absolutely certain?'

'Yes, I am.'

'And if I told you that the name Aino does not exist, that I dreamed it up, that it's my invention, what would you say then?'

'I would say that you may very well have made it up, but that it existed before then and you were unaware of it.'

'Why won't you admit that there was no discussion, no seminar?'

'Because there was.'

'Why won't you admit that all you fancy archaeologists haven't the least idea what Aino means. Why do you insist on annoying me in this way?'

'It is not my intention to annoy you,' I said with uncharacteristic honesty. I was close to tears.

'You're an intelligent human being,' he said, 'but you cannot escape the idiocy of youth. Perhaps I was a little hasty, and should have arranged to meet you ten years hence.'

I stopped talking. I was offended, even though I knew he was right. I wished I could tell him everything, how I was drawn into a web of lies without realising it, that I was sorry, but I didn't, I just kept silent.

'I am angry, not because of your appalling pride, that's not such a serious vice really, I am angry because I had wanted to share something important with you, and you have betrayed my expectations of you.'

I could have told him that he was partly responsible for the fact that I was forced into such stupid behaviour and that it was he who had led me to the pettiness that he was now condemning me for. But I didn't dare.

'I would like to believe that you are not an entirely

hopeless case. But at this precise moment, there is nothing I wish to discuss with you. You had better go now, and get some rest.'

I replaced the hurricane lamp and heard him call behind me:

'For yesterday, however, I am grateful.'

And then, as if an insect had stung him:

'Run along now, won't you. Let's not let the day go to waste.'

In the midst of my confusion, instead of moving towards the door, I tried to leave via the balcony. When I tried to turn the knob I became aware of my mistake, but attempted to conceal it so I flung open the double doors, and stepped out onto the roof terrace. I walked right up to the edge, trying to make it seem that I wanted to get some air, or that I wanted to take a close look at the trees. I stayed there for five, perhaps ten, minutes.

I turned round and walked back into Argyriadis's room and left through the correct door without saying a word.

I felt his puzzled gaze follow me out of the room.

eighteen

You'd never guess that the Aino backed onto a substantial piece of land, a walled-off garden which was not visible either from the main road or from the small street running down the side of the building. Tended exclusively by Mother Nature, the garden gave the impression of once belonging to a far-away forest and that one beautiful morning it had detached itself and appeared inexplicably in the midst of this built-up area. Some of the trees were old and tall, but it was quite a job trying to work out what species each one was because of the way they knotted themselves together with the result that the branches of one tree looked like they had sprouted from the trunk of another. In one corner there was a crop of irises in bloom, yellow and purple, a handful of stray bulbs performing a miracle. Other, more humble flowers made an appearance too, most of them around the perimeter of the garden, beyond the reach of the shade of the trees. So if you edited out the odd discarded tin can and the inelegant exteriors of the surrounding buildings from your field of vision, the picture was idyllic. You almost expected some sluggish tortoise to come lumbering up to you, or a lithe, fluffy little polecat. It gave you a good idea of what the area had been like only a few decades back. How else could you explain those tall trees, if not as part of an enormous forest, decimated over time?

The image of the mute woman stealing eggs from the birds' nests sprang to mind once again.

At the entrance to the forest garden, a large rectangular cage stood on the ground. Its long side must have been at least a metre and a half. Unsurprisingly it was empty, but on closer inspection you could see the semi-petrified traces of feathers. My knowledge of the history of the hotel was admittedly sketchy, but it was hard to imagine who had put the cage in the garden. Filippos Argyriadis hated birds – that much I did know. I doubt whether Argyriadis *père* was similarly sensitive and I'm absolutely sure that the mute wasn't. The image of that cage sitting there, in that particular spot, empty though it was, intensified the impression I had of the scene, one I'm at a loss to clarify with the help of mere words.

One evening, as I was leaving the garden to go up to my room, I noticed a huge crack on the back wall of the building, probably the work of some earthquake. A snake-like line, it started high up at the top, working its way down diagonally, until it disappeared into the foliage of an ivy, which for reasons of its own, chose not to climb up the wall but to crawl along the ground instead. Following the course of the crack with my eye, I discovered a fanlight, just above ground level, an *œil-de-bœuf*, dark and half-concealed by the ivy, slightly above ground level, which suggests that it was designed to let light into a basement room. That's how I discovered the existence of the basement. It was just as serendipitous as my discovery of the lumber-room had been.

I was almost certain that the entrance to the basement was through one of the restaurants facing the street, not through the Aino. I knew the layout of the ground floor well: the

Oeil-de-bœuf

reception area can't have been more than ten square metres, the small lounge twenty at most, and as for Stelios and his father's room – I'd been inside a couple of times – I was certain that there weren't any other doors that could lead to a basement. Besides, it stood to reason that the restaurants would have some kind of storage area at their disposal for those bulky umbrellas, tables and chairs that colonised the pavements during the summer months.

I could have asked Stelios about some of this, about the cage in the garden for example, but he had been keeping his distance. He was avoiding me, and I noticed how he would frequently abandon his post and dash into his room as soon as he heard me coming down the stairs. I didn't like it; it puzzled me, and made me think that the most plausible explanation was that he was acting on his father's orders.

I thought that was the reason because I had eavesdropped on a conversation they had one day when their door was ajar. As usual, father was giving son a good dressing down. His voice was lowered almost to a whisper, each consonant voiced so emphatically that all his sounds were perfectly formed, making what he said just as audible as if he had been shouting. Admittedly, I didn't hear myself mentioned by name; I didn't have to. He said:

'It's not your job to go engaging people in conversation, your job is to keep your mouth shut. Don't let me catch you chatting away with him again. Watch it, son! Do as I do – be polite to everyone, but always know what to say and what not to say. And when you don't have a clue what you shouldn't be saying, it's best to keep your mouth shut.'

Stelios, as usual, said nothing. They emerged from their room, and the father put on a fake smile as soon as he saw me, came up to me, greeted me with a supposedly heartfelt handshake while Stelios hung back, burnt.

'If only you knew how much Mr Argyriadis respects you,' he said. 'Only this morning he was asking me if you were happily settled here, and if there was anything we could do to make you more comfortable. Don't hesitate to let us know if there's anything you need. How do you find the food over there?'

They had arranged for me to take my meals at one of the downstairs restaurants. I assured him that everything was fine. Later, he produced his accounts book and pretended to be busy, but I could see him observing me through the corner of his eye.

Trusty old dog. Blind in his devotion to old Argyriadis until the day of his death, a regular Cerberus, guarding all his secrets and shady affairs. And then he transferred to the service of Filippos Argyriadis with the same devotion, passing on to his own son the values of subordination, the duty to respect and protect your employer. If anyone concluded that he was a smarmy character, judging by his cunning affectations and his fake civility, they would be missing the point that here was a being capable of the greatest sacrifice – if his employer required it – a rare virtue these days.

But stranger than that was the way that Stelios had adopted this virtue. I can't say whether this was a result of so much exposure to his father or the outcome of some sort of genetic transfer, but it was not what you would expect from a young man who should, all things being equal, want to shake off all forms of limitation and coercion. Stelios had swallowed the entire mentality. It was not until much later that I realised this. His devotion to Filippos Argyriadis was unshakeable. He lacked the necessary skills to get on in life, he was crude and unrefined but would never betray the trust of his boss, even on pain of death.

But despite their obvious loyalty, they were in no way servile. Far from it. They considered themselves to be an integral part of the place, which made them inordinately self-confident, something akin to the arrogance of a head waiter in a high-class restaurant. I remember how Stelios's father used to boss the cleaner and the chambermaid around, ordering them to sweep the entrance or put fresh towels in one of the rooms in such an authoritarian manner that you'd be forgiven for thinking he was the managing director of some huge multinational concern.

I have no idea what Stelios's mother's story might be, no idea why Stelios ended up being raised by his father. The situation bore traces of the Argyriadis family arrangements. I never did find out, I never had the nerve to come straight out and ask.

The first time I went to their room Stelios had invited me in to show me his cowboy boots. I was amazed at how neat and tidy the place was. There was a bed against one wall, and another against the opposite wall. At the far end of the large room (well, it was certainly bigger than the lounge outside) there was a window looking back out on to the garden. Underneath it was a metal desk, standard school issue, supporting a whole host of things neatly piled on top of it. Stelios had put some pictures torn out of magazines up on his side of the room. Some colour, some black and white (rock stars, naked women) in what appeared to be a jigsaw arrangement. Looking across the room at them were his father's holy icons of the saints.

On the other wall, the wall with the door, there was an enormous wardrobe covered in dark gloss paint. Five doors, holding all their worldly goods.

Father and son spent their entire life in that room.

It occurred to me that there might be another reason why Stelios was giving me the cold shoulder all of a sudden. There was a girl who visited him; I assumed she was his girlfriend. The first time I saw her I was with Stelios down at reception. She had turned up carrying a bunch of flowers. He didn't introduce us. The girl looked at me intently and then, without hesitation they disappeared into the room. I left after that and have no idea how long they spent in there. The second time I saw her she was walking into the hotel just as I was coming down the stairs. Because I didn't want to put her or anyone else in a difficult position again, I held back – I was still quite near the top – to give her enough time to get inside and avoid an embarrassing encounter. But instead of taking advantage of it, she just stood there, looking at me. Not just looking, piercing me with her gaze and making me feel very uncomfortable. She was carrying a spray of flowering lilac. I had no choice but to greet her and make my way downstairs. She gave a brief nod and vanished into the room with Stelios. Beautiful eyes. Simos Skouris was waiting for me down in the lounge, and started his volley of questions, so there wasn't any time for me to process the incident. Only later, when I noticed the change in Stelios's attitude to me, did it occur to me that if indeed she was his girlfriend, and if indeed the poor chap had picked up on the fact that she was interested in me, perhaps his irritation was justified.

But it wasn't like that at all.

NINeteen

In the twilight zone between sleep and wakefulness, when I start to slip into the territory of the unconscious, but have not lost all connection with the here and now, in the intermediate phase of a few moments, I realise that two strange things are happening. The first is that if I hear a piece of music or a song in the distance, from a radio in the next door room, or a nearby television set, the tune will provoke a profound sense of exultation in me, as though the music issued from the spheres, music that if I heard it at any other time, might have been totally indifferent to me. For some reason, it seems that while I am on the borderline, hovering between the two states, the impact of all music on me is pervasive.

The other strange thing: if a memory comes to me, bringing to life an old image, distance and time are erased. I am transported right back to it, I relive that time and space. I'm not daydreaming, my conscience, my senses, all march to the beat of the vanished moment. But don't a lot of people maintain that they are able to revisit the past with the help of hypnosis? I wonder whether something similar happens to me when I'm in that semi-hypnotic state. Unfortunately, because my consciousness is still active to a degree, this transference startles me, wakes me up, and it's all over. I'm back in the present. Very rarely, I manage to stay asleep, and before long, reliving the past merges with dreaming proper. (I'd love the chance to discuss all this with a specialist.)

That's how I was a short while ago, sitting in my armchair, reading through everything I'd written so far about the copse behind the Aino. I was tired and just as I was dozing off, found myself among its tall trees, with dazzling sunlight shining on all creation from behind the clouds. And that's when the incident with the cat hit me like a thunderclap.

It was a tabby cat; its markings reminded me of the arrangement of the scales on certain fish, club mackerel, possibly. She was a gentle creature, very gentle, poor thing. She'd wander round the hotel, snuggling up to anyone who paid her any attention. I often saw her taking a nap on a rug, or taking a walk in the garden. She kept away from the street. She didn't belong to anyone, she just turned up at the Aino one day and installed herself there. Stelios gave her food – for a few days at least; she wasn't around much longer than that.

One morning I was woken by Filippos Argyriadis, screaming at Stelios, his shouts punctuated by Stelios's father who was outdoing Argyriadis, repeating the same phrase over and over: 'You animal! You animal!' At first I didn't have a clue what was going on.

Stelios sometimes let a dog in, and let him have some of the restaurant leftovers. The cat couldn't stand the dog, and whenever he charged after her, she'd be up in the highest branches like a shot. It seemed that on that fateful evening (encouraged perhaps by hunger as Stelios had forgotten to feed her) she decided to put on a show of bravado and sidled up to the spot where the dog was eating, hoping to swipe a piece of meat.

'I'd put her food out on her plate. I forgot to give it her, that's all,' said Stelios in a funereal voice.

'Animal! Animal!'

It didn't take much for disaster to strike. It hardly ever does. As soon as the dog got wind of what the cat was up to, he pounced on her, ripped her to shreds, making short work of her. The body was not discovered until the following day. There were witnesses though, I was one, who had heard the primal howl of an animal, a bark coming from the mouth of a cat.

'Where was she? Where did you find her?' screamed the collector.

'Under the poplar,' came the subdued admission of the guilty party. 'Her throat was punctured and tufts of her fur were scattered all over the place. Her ear was shredded. And there was a wound on her leg.'

His honesty was admirable, considering what a difficult position he was in. But forgetting to feed the cat and causing the dog to attack her were not his only mistakes; he was responsible for something else. Something even more serious. The following day, when he discovered the cat's lifeless body under the poplar, he had put it in a plastic bag and tossed it into the municipal rubbish bin.

'You can't get any sicker than that,' thundered Argyriadis. 'Are you completely devoid of sensitivity? How could you just toss the cat into the rubbish?'

'I scooped her up by the tail with a newspaper and stuffed the body into the bag,' answered Stelios steadily, failing to realise that the truth has the capacity to undermine us.

'Animal! You threw the cat onto the rubbish?' echoed his father, by now incandescent – although I half suspect that he would have done just that in his son's position.

'I'm speechless. Didn't it occur to you that we could have buried her at the bottom of the garden? Get out of my sight. I don't want to see your face round here again – at least not for a week.' And with that parting shot, Filippos Argyriadis walked off.

Although he said nothing, Stelios was clearly shaken by the episode. His father patted him on the head, whispering some 'it doesn't matters' and 'it'll be all rights' in his ear. If his boss hadn't got so incensed by the event, he would never have become exercised by it, hardened by life as he was. He would never have attacked his son on account of a dead cat. Dogs have always gone for cats and always would. A lot of nonsense – it was just the law of nature, and so what if people tossed them on the rubbish afterwards? The paternal caress, the straw that broke the camel's back, had Stelios briefly in tears. He quickly pulled himself together, wiped his eyes, and within a matter of half a minute, both men had resumed their normal rhythms.

Of course none of this would ever have happened in front of me. I observed the entire scene from the top of the staircase, played out in the big mirror hanging in the entrance across from the reception desk.

twenty

This is the twentieth time I have sat down to write in this notebook. Almost two months have passed since I started. Sometimes I question the point of it. As I said in the first place, I will succeed in rescuing a few details from oblivion, and perhaps judge my own role in all this by putting everything that took place down on paper. There always comes a point though when I want to stop, and not go on any further. I'm often tempted to tear up the notebook, and put this dilemma to rest once and for all. But I don't. A few days go by and I come back to it, the way a murderer returns to the scene of the crime. That's when I realise how difficult it is for me to get to the heart of the matter, I make my way forward with lopsided steps, forever inserting parentheses, one after the other – and dashes – I walk around the issue, never quite ready to start the countdown. Perhaps I should have taken a different starting point. It's not too late to remedy that. Quite simply, when I get to the end (if indeed I ever do), and have everything down on paper, I can shift things around a bit. Copy out the events in a different order. Surely it must be possible to write a novel like that too? A novel destined for one and only one reader: the author himself. Myself, that is. One way of doing it would be to kick off with Aliki, the girl

I saw staring at me penetratingly at the Aino reception, the one I mistook for Stelios's girlfriend.

A fresh bouquet of flowers and two damp eyes staring right into the depths of my soul – my first memory of the ghost-girl in the hotel reception.

Not a bad opening at all, is it? I could present Aliki as a vision, perhaps a figment of my imagination, and then I'd leave her, go on to a description of the five links in the chain, and then I'd reintroduce her towards the end, to explain her visits to the Aino. For this scene I would use everything that was said during my own meeting with her at the restaurant – I haven't got round to that yet – with the only difference that I would have staged the meeting in a much more poetic setting, on the edge of a rock with the sea behind her.

But I could have given the hotel itself a much stronger aura of mystery if I'd wanted to, if I had described it as a tower, standing in some out of the way place, indistinct in the fog.

Let's stick to the facts for the moment, and to Aliki while we're on the subject. Yes. It really did strike me as inconceivable that she was having an affair with Stelios, but what was I supposed to think each time she turned up with a bunch of flowers and disappeared into his room with him? It wasn't that she was beautiful, she was extraordinary. The overall impression of her features was very unusual. I'm not saying that Stelios was ugly or anything like that – he had a certain style that a lot of women would find attractive. It was just that it seemed so unlikely, so unnatural that those two should be a couple, rather like a butterfly consorting with a cicada.

The first time I saw her, she confused me. I found it quite impossible to form any impression of her at all. I couldn't even decide whether she was beautiful or ugly, whether I liked her or not, whether she was older or younger than me.

All I knew was that I had been blinded by an intense ray of light – so sudden and so unexpected that I was unable to make any observations or draw any conclusions about her at all. It was only later, much later, that my impression of her assumed any substance. And now, with the benefit of hindsight, it is clearer than ever. There was something trashy about her. Scruffy jeans, too many earrings, close-cropped boyish hair. No make-up, although sometimes she looked made up even without it. Long, slender fingers, full of rings, which in combination with the rest of her appearance, made you think that they'd had more practice filching wallets than playing the piano or the guitar. There was also a strength about her, a strength in her eyes; unused to compromise.

At the same time, she had some other features which contradicted this impression. Her neck was long, and the way she carried herself spoke of a girl from another era, brought up by her governess and ballet instructor. Her movements were elegant, her voice, when I eventually heard it, was soft and sweet. None of this gelled with the trashy aspects. You get that sometimes in the cinema – the heroine starts off as wretched, suffering perpetual hardships, but you guess how things are going to develop and start noticing details about her, hints of beauty and glamour, which pave the way for her transformation after the intermission. Beneath her trashy exterior I saw another, hidden Aliki – it was never revealed to me but I'm convinced it was there.

When I met Aliki, her life was going from bad to worse. Bad luck was responsible for some of it; bad judgement for the rest. Pity! Such a nice creature but I just stood there doing nothing, watching her destruction in silence. I never once tried to help her. I'm not proud of that. But back then, I was far too absorbed in my own problems. I never did hear what happened to her. Could be a good sign, on the other hand, it could also be a bad sign. I promise myself that I will try to find out what has become of her, because she did so much for me, and I really hope nothing has happened to her.

I'm going to leave Aliki to one side for a while; it was a mistake to start talking about her. I'll gather my thoughts together, and first thing tomorrow I'll return to the main story, starting with how I came to find out the meaning of the name Aino.

twenty-one

I found out quite by chance; through a mistake or rather a piece of idiocy on the part of Simos Skouris. It seems that just before our group meeting on the roof terrace, the sect had assembled and Argyriadis told them that he was intending to see me the following morning at ten to let me in on the Aino secret. Obviously Skouris did not suspect and certainly wasn't informed of our disaster of a meeting, and went away with the impression that Argyriadis had already told me. That explains why he kept flashing that cunning little smile of his at me when we saw each other a few hours later (he had seen to it that he would be the first to see me after the supposed revelation). I hadn't a clue why he was doing that; I assumed it was somehow related to my confession of the night before. But I was not confused for long as Skouris came out with it almost immediately.

'So how does it feel, now that you know all about Aino? It could change your life forever, couldn't it?'

I didn't dare confess to the earlier fiasco. I was stunned, said nothing and waited for him to continue.

'I can see why you might have some reservations. Perhaps you don't quite believe what you've been told, you're not sure whether the information is reliable. Rest assured, it all checks out. There's proof. Go on, celebrate! As of today, you are in possession of some rare, unique knowledge.'

That was it. This was driving me insane. But I kept my wits about me and tried to manoeuvre Skouris into spilling the beans before he suspected the truth.

'It still hasn't quite sunk in. I must admit I am still very confused by it all.'

'Confused? In what sense?'

I realised that 'confused' was the wrong angle.

'Oh – it's all so new to me,' I ventured.

He shot me a patronising smile.

'Almost unbelievable.'

He nodded; I was back on track.

'Exactly,' he said. 'Aino has managed to remain dark and mysterious, just the way she wanted it.'

'Where did it all start?' Without really knowing what I was asking, I had stumbled on the key, the cue Skouris was waiting for, a sign to start talking. I frequently had trouble following him, but my queries were usually cleared up a few minutes later by another thread. Through close attention to everything he said, I was able to perform my role as interlocutor quite convincingly, although our conversation was essentially a monologue. But by the end of it, I had found out everything, well, at least the essentials.

Aino was an ancient Greek deity. A daughter of Zeus. The protector of secrets. She was worshipped just as the other better-known gods were, only nothing was ever known about her. Why was that? Quite simply, that was the way she wanted it. It was forbidden to write her name, to create images of her, or statues of her. It was even forbidden to utter her name at gatherings or in public places. Only at strictly private gatherings was it permissible, which is how her cult survived at all. Violations were punished harshly: the secrets of those responsible were exposed. Not surprisingly, this proved an effective deterrent. People have always had something to hide. It explains why no evidence of her cult has ever been found. From time to time, and this happens throughout history, there were a few people who wanted to break the code of silence. Particularly those whose secrets had already been revealed, people who had had confidences betrayed, people who had nothing to lose and who held the goddess, the very power that was supposed to protect them, culpable for these disasters. Embittered and enraged, they created statues of her, engraving her name at the base, they drew pictures of her, and so on. But not even this evidence survived for long, because as soon as such images came to the attention of anyone else, they were destroyed, because everyone else was duty-bound to preserve her anonymity, and this duty extended beyond merely remaining silent to destroying any evidence they came across. Otherwise there was a risk of suffering the unpleasant consequences of exposure. Skouris even told me what she looked like. Her face was balanced, beautiful, but had no lips or mouth. The area beneath her nose was occupied by a gap.

I'm getting confused, and I can't remember at which point I found out what, while I was sounding out Simos Skouris, and what I discovered subsequently. Not that it matters much. Anyway, that's how I found out about Aino, in the funniest and most unexpected way imaginable. If somebody had been listening in on that conversation, they would have cracked up laughing: how a wily young man managed to pull the wool over the eyes of a naïve, middle-aged intellectual was the stuff of hilarious comedy. But to me, the only person who could have been aware of the comic dimensions of the situation, laughter was the furthest thing from my mind. In a state of near shock, I tried to gather up the words thrown my way by the unsuspecting Skouris, and as the tiny pieces of the mosaic began to fall into place, however vaguely, the more I felt cast adrift in a sea of confusion.

Realising that I'd squeezed every last drop out of my informer, I suddenly felt the need to be by myself. I needed to enjoy the luscious fruit I'd plucked from the tree alone. I needed to consider every detail carefully and think where I might be able to find evidence for it and what I could do with this treasure house of information that had fallen into my hands. Grateful though I was to Simos Skouris, it was quite impossible for me, in my present state, to tolerate his incessant talking any longer. It was as though some god somewhere had heard my prayer; just then the most deafening racket erupted outside in the street, the voices and shouts of a crowd getting denser by the minute, climaxing with the sound of the municipal band. We were forced to break off our conversation. I ran up to my room and locked the door.

My stomach was a huge heap of knots. My brain was beating against my skull like a racing pulse. A goddess who was completely unheard of! An object of worship – every last trace of her covered up down the centuries. I'm sure that even if I hadn't been an archaeology student, I would have been just as excited. The voices in the street below, and the paens seemed to be celebrating the news. I looked out of the window. Through a small opening in the trees I could see that the band had set up in the square a little further along from the shopping centre. A lot of people were making their way across; obviously some sort of festivities were due to begin. I went down into the street and joined them. It was something to do, a release of sorts.

They were putting on some sort of show in honour of the former mayor, for the anniversary, I'm not sure which, of his death. He'd served for a great many years and was extremely popular. The highlight of the event was the unveiling of his statue in the main square. It was ages since I had been among people; living in the hotel was like living in quarantine. I could picture myself going up to people, grabbing them by the hand and telling them everything about Aino, Goddess of secrets. I'd be taken for a lunatic.

The speeches were about to start. They'd put up a platform complete with sound system. But the sound waves didn't seem to be entering through my ears; they were exploding inside my temples and rebounding. Simos Skouris's phrase was spinning in my head, constantly, 'Don't worry, there is evidence for all of this!' I hoped so, because without it this charming story would never be more than a charming story. I had to wonder what kind of evidence the sect had in its possession when archaeologists had been kept in the dark for centuries. These concerns put a damper on my original enthusiasm; I feared that the entire Aino story was no more than the product of an eccentric imagination. And something else occurred to me: in case everything I had been told was true and I managed to prove it, it would have enormous consequences for the career of a young archaeologist who hadn't even graduated yet. It would be huge. Immediately afterwards (the former mayor's widow had stepped up onto the podium) I had to question why it had been kept secret for so long, why Filippos Argyriadis hadn't taken advantage of this knowledge, settling instead for naming his hotel after the vanished goddess. What else didn't I know?

As my eye hovered idly across the unfamiliar faces in the crowd (my sight as well as my hearing had been neutralised by my over-active thoughts), something jolted me awake like a sudden cold shower. I spotted a pair of eyes fixed on me; they could have been staring at me long before I noticed them. Like strong projector lights, they cut through the distance and through any foreign bodies that happened to be standing between us. Filippos Argyriadis. He was standing only a few metres away from me, at the refreshments stand, half-hidden by the backs of the serving staff tirelessly filling and refilling plastic cups. My embarrassment was just as intense as my sense of surprise because I had been standing there with the lack of self-consciousness anonymity allows us, and have no idea what sort of inane expression I had, lost in my thoughts as I was. Totally spontaneously, I raised my hand to greet him. My greeting was exaggerated but natural enough for someone trying to get noticed in a crowd of people, bearing in mind, however, the recent strained atmosphere, it was perhaps incompatible. Argyriadis, more in keeping with this atmosphere, simply nodded.

I started to make my way towards him through the crowd. My mind was made up: no more lying, no more strategies, no more hypocrisy. From that moment forward I was going to put my cards on the table. No more games.

'Mr Argyriadis, please forgive me for spoiling your mood this morning,' I said loudly enough to make myself heard. 'I hope we can put all that behind us now.'

Then I pulled him slightly to one side:

'I have just been made aware of everything connected with Aino; Mr Skouris has told me everything. Please, no, don't be annoyed with him,' I said hurriedly, seeing his pupils suddenly flash in anger. 'He isn't to blame; he thought you had already told me. If anyone is to blame in all this it is I. I made no attempt to disabuse him of this notion and I encouraged him to talk. I couldn't help myself; only some kind of superman could have resisted, or a saint. The fact is that I now know everything there is to know about the unknown goddess of secrets.'

I had barely got to the end of my sentence when the crowd broke into a hearty round of applause. The incumbent mayor had just pulled back the burlap covering the marble bust and the band struck up a joyful march. We both turned to watch as it was impossible to continue our conversation, and stood there for a while. Standing side by side, like common spectators, without looking at each other, but maintaining some sort of communication even so.

During this brief silence, it occurred to me that (Paraschis had told me this earlier) at the same place where the ceremony was taking place, long before either the shopping centre or the square had been built, there had been a small pine grove where Argyriadis *père* and the starving girl, the collector's mother, first met. Only one large pine tree on the edge of the square had survived.

Something else occurred to me on the tail of that thought; as the mouthless goddess, so the unfortunate woman: created for, or rather condemned to, silence. Of course she did have a mouth. But not for talking with. Only for eating.

twenty-two

'Come on, let's go,' he said after a while, tapping me gently on the shoulder.

We walked into the Aino, up to the roof terrace. My heart was pounding, his too, I imagine. It took a long time to explain things as he demanded a blow-by-blow account of how it had come about that Simos Skouris could have committed such a monumental blunder. I remember accepting the blame for the entire business, but that didn't seem to soften his irritation with the goldsmith-poet in the least.

I in turn begged him to explain everything to me from the beginning, even though I had already heard most of it. It was incredible how different it all sounded coming from Argyriadis. His voice, as always, starting out from its dark, hoarse regions, slowly rising in line with the intensity of the emotion expressed to more crystalline, though always faltering, frequencies. His deep blue eyes shone as I seized every word coming out of his mouth like a greedy fledgling. He didn't flag at any point, all his sentences were pithy and well-turned, his syntax commanding. His speech did not bear the marks of improvisation typical of spoken discourse, it gave you more the impression that he was reading out loud from the pages of a book.

At the end of the first section, which could have gone by the title 'Who was Aino?', he stopped to come up for air, and I took the opportunity to ask him about what had been on my mind for so long: How had he come by all this information in the first place, and how reliable was it?

'My father...' he began and then shot me an irresolute glance, trying to decide whether to go ahead with this confidence or not. But he was swept away by the internal rhythms of his own speech. 'He was uncompromising. Even if he had been thrown to the bottom of a dry well, he would have survived. Invulnerable. Through all those difficult times, he was always one step ahead, and knew exactly how to protect himself. Nothing touched him, acts of God, upheavals, wars, nothing. He was immune to it all. Of course a lot of people despised him for it. Can't say I blame them. His desire to prevail at all time often made him inhuman. I was able to forgive him for his abuses, not because he was my father, but because I understood that it couldn't be helped. It was an irresistible drive, a natural urge which he could do nothing about. Nobody resents the lion at the moment he punctures the flesh of the innocent gazelle, do they? My father was surrounded by gazelles who were happy to place their necks directly inside the lion's jaw, without any encouragement.'

'I don't follow.'

'When times were hard, desperate people came running to Argyriadis for help. When food was in short supply, there was no shortage of people willing to trade something valuable for a crust of bread. My father went along with it, believing that this kind of trade off achieved a stay of execution for a few doomed souls. Bear in mind that the streets were littered with dead bodies at the time.'

I couldn't tell if Filippos Argyriadis himself espoused the

logic of the blackmarketeer. I somehow doubted it. But it wasn't the time to get into a discussion of this kind. I made a point of not commenting on what he said.

'For the most part it was jewellery, more rarely old coins. One piece, however, whose value nobody suspected at the time, fell into my hands shortly before my father's death. It was an old document, a Byzantine codex. A nine-leaf signature – thirty-six pages in all. Nobody knows what monastery it came from, or indeed how it ended up in the possession of some unfortunate peasant who decided to hand it over to my father rather than die of starvation. My father wasn't particularly excited about it; it just lay there for years forgotten in a packing case along with various journals and almanacs. It was a stroke of luck that it never shared the fate of that poor cat. A magnificent manuscript, a psalter. When I set about restoring it, I discovered that it was actually some kind of palimpsest. The psalms were copied onto Arabic paper, stuck on top with a plant gum over the original parchment of the codex. What's more, the original parchment leaves also contained an older text. At a rough guess, the codex was written and bound during the 10th century (the script was all lower case). The psalms might have been added one hundred, maybe two hundred years later. After that, I immediately called on the help of an old palaeographer friend of mine; sadly he passed away a few years ago. He also did excellent conservation work. Together we managed to remove the top layer of paper to reveal the original document that had been lying there undisturbed for hundreds of years.

'The text. Let's turn to the text. It was a sketch of three female figures from antiquity. There might have been other volumes that made up part of a series dealing with other figures from antiquity. We just don't know. The first words of the work, the title if you prefer, consisted of the three female names, Rhea, Hera and Aino. Now, it didn't tell us anything we didn't already know about Rhea and Hera – not that that detracted from the near-mystical experience of reading the text. The last section, the section dealing with Aino, was quite literally the key opening the door to this ancient, secret gate. Through those lines all the extraordinary information you heard earlier for the first time from me jumped out from the page at me.' (Apparently he wanted to overlook the fact that I had already heard everything from Simos Skouris.)

He went on:

'The author, after describing the goddess, discusses the serious matter of the code of silence and how it worked as a deterrent to all those tempted to open their mouths. He talked ironically about the readiness with which the ancients succumbed to this terrifying superstition which, as he makes clear, has been forgotten for centuries now. In a footnote at the end of the main text, on the last page, written in italics, he adds that he no longer feared that anyone else would try to destroy his text, as had clearly happened a few hundred years earlier, for the simple reason that his text talked about Aino. It seems that he was confident that the human spirit had made progress since then.'

'But somebody did write over it, with those psalms a century later,' I objected, 'I bet that whoever it was had an entire closet full of skeletons.'

'I must confess that neither my restorer friend nor I took it at all seriously. My first reaction was that the author was indulging in some literary game, that he was some joker of a scribe, looking for a little light relief during those endless hours of copying, or else he was trying to play a trick on subsequent scholars, by inventing this tale, slyly incorporating it into other pieces of established information, the passages about Rhea and Hera, to make it look more convincing. That's what I thought. Anyway, I was sure that the scribe was a young man; I could tell from the pressure he applied to the pen as he wrote, and the speed at which the words were forged, not to mention the many omissions of aspirant and other accents, missing syllables and ink spills. I immediately ran to all the dictionaries and encyclopaedias I could find, anyone would have done the same – but came up with nothing. In Stamatakos's *Lexicon of The Ancient Greek Language* I came across the extremely rare adjective "αινός αινή αινόν," meaning "harsh, frightening, terrible" and frequently used to describe Zeus, Aino's father, in other words. Semantically, there could be a link between the adjective and the name of what the codex described as this harsh, threatening figure, without that necessarily meaning anything or proving anything.'

'Rhea, Hera and Aino,' I whispered, belatedly considering all the relations to Zeus there: mother, wife and daughter.

Filippos Argyriadis blinked and continued:

'I don't have to tell you how proud I was of my new acquisition, even though deep down I was convinced that the Aino text was bogus, but that didn't prevent the codex from being of enormous historical and financial value.'

'And then a year later, I was touring the Asia Minor coast. I was walking around one of the local museums when I suddenly noticed an exhibit, and found it hard to contain myself. It was a struggle to hold back the tears. A small rectangular stone plaque was on display along with several others in the same case. In the middle of it there was a crudely drawn face, without any lips, accompanied by the phrase "ΟΥ ΦΟΒΗΣΟΜΑΙ ΑΙΝΩ ΟΝΟΜΑΣΑΙ" – "I will not fear to speak the name Aino". The word "Aino" was slightly worn and hard to make out, but the number of letters was obvious, four, as were the traces of the *nu* and the *omega*. The other words were clear. It wouldn't have surprised me if the wear and tear to the word Aino was not accidental.'

He went on:

'Yes. That's when I began to research, as systematically as I could, the world's museums. My efforts were rewarded by another discovery. In the Munich museum there's a perfectly preserved ceramic pot dating back to the Classical period, a cup, and on its bowl there is a female form without a mouth. Three words are written above her head: "ΚΡΥΦΙΑ ΔΕΙΝΗ ΑΕΘΩΝΙΑ" – "Secret, awe-inspiring Aethonia."'

'Aethonia?' I said.

'Haven't you worked it out?' he smiled. 'If you saw it written down, I'm sure you'd get it right away. It's an anagram: Aethonia: *Aino thea* – goddess Aino.'

And after the briefest pause:

'That was enough for me. I broke off my research. There was no point – I had all the confirmation I needed. I'm sure there is more proof out there. But it's not my job to find it. It's yours. It's up to the archaeologists to find everything that escaped the divine injunction, everything that escaped destruction. Do you realise that the proof of the codex, the proof that confirms the existence of the cult of the unknown goddess, is not in my possession, it's out there, in the world's museums, under the very noses of you expert archaeologists.' (His irony did not escape me.) 'But they don't hold the key to the interpretation of the evidence. I do. It's in this palimpsest.'

I latched onto the last thing he said and asked why he hadn't gone public with the codex; how did keeping it hidden benefit him?

'Hasn't it occurred to you that I might be just a little wary of divine retribution? That perhaps I have secrets which I would not risk coming out for anything in the world?'

I couldn't tell whether he was saying all this in jest or not.

'Haven't you considered the possibility that I am trembling

as we speak?'

I began to suspect that he was not talking in jest.

'Imagine what danger I'd be in if I were the cause of Aino ending up as front page news? Never. I would never dare publish anything about her. Would you?'

'Yes, yes I would,' I said without hesitation.

'Before you go rushing into such an unconsidered response, remember that you too have a secret – at least one as far as I know. And you don't want that getting out, do you? Don't forget: secrets govern our lives.'

My initial reaction was to laugh. Awkward laughter.

'I've never seen you laugh before. Why don't you laugh more?

It was approximately at that point that our conversation came to an end.

TUESDAY, 23RD NOVEMBER 1999

I want to turn to the present now, to the events of this evening when, after eight years, I went back to the Aino.

I should add that on none of my short visits home from Italy, did I ever have the courage to walk past the place casually, or even to drive past in a car. In the three months I've been back, the thought has often flickered through my mind, but never got any further than that.

This morning was different. I was overwhelmed by the urge to stand in front of that building again, to see its broad facade choked by leaves, to see how my own memory of it stood up to the real thing. And if I was lucky, experience that smell again.

I waited for it to get dark; I didn't want to be spotted. I had no idea what things were like round there these days, as I'd stopped asking years ago. I borrowed a motorcycle helmet, which I slipped onto my head as I soon as I got out of the taxi – one street further down to avoid any chance encounters. I approached the building confident that everything would be just as I had left it.

But nothing was. To begin with, the Aino had gone. Sure, the building was still standing, but the hotel where I'd spent an entire fortnight, Filippos Argyriadis's hotel, was a thing of the past.

One of the downstairs restaurants had been taken over by a hideous new enterprise which spread up to the floor above as well, sectioned off into different entertainment areas. The ground floor was a cafeteria, open all day, serving overpriced cakes and sandwiches. The upstairs, the Aino in other words, had been turned into a luxury restaurant, only operating in the evening. The basement, that basement, was now an Internet café with giant screens all across the walls, showing non-stop music videos. The only trace of its former identity was the circular fanlight, the ivy-choked *œil de bœuf* I'd stumbled across quite by chance in the garden. A summer bar had opened on the roof terrace; all of these businesses operated under the umbrella name Alabaster. Terrible.

Fortunately, the trees which used to shade the upper floor were still standing, but had fallen victim to the most extreme attack of pruning I'd ever seen. The back garden, which had resembled a jungle back then, was also tamed and contained the overspill of the tables from the ground floor café. The new regime had gone to great lengths to exploit every last square inch of space, and had managed to extinguish all traces of the old atmosphere. Everything had changed beyond recognition.

Eventually I realised I could safely remove the helmet without running the risk of being recognised; these new brooms would certainly have driven out the old ghosts. My initial reaction to the Alabaster was undiluted hostility but it now struck me as a perfectly innocuous, unsuspecting (and why wouldn't it be?) and hospitable place. I thought that if I waited a little, half an hour or so, I could have dinner at the restaurant and take the opportunity to study the various changes to the interior at my leisure, which is exactly what I did.

As soon as I got to the first floor – the beautiful old wooden staircase had been ripped out and replaced with a metal one –

I was shocked to see how the space had been modified. All the internal walls had been knocked down, all the walls separating the bedrooms. They'd opened up one enormous central area, divided only by occasional glass panels, lit diagonally from underneath by some hidden fittings, creating soft iridescent pools of light. The walls were painted an undulating peach and some of the balcony doors of the bedrooms had been bricked in half way up and made into ordinary windows; the rest had been closed up altogether.

Holding on to the image of the old hotel layout in my mind, I tried to get my bearings. Looking down, with my focus more on the combination of mosaic and parquet flooring, I tried to locate the places that led to the rooms – the corridor and the toilets – but it was too confusing. The new layout threw me. It was only the windows, and the view of the street below that gave me a sense of where I was. They acted as reference points, helping me recreate the old environment in just the same way a smile can help you put a name to a long-forgotten face. I searched around for the doorway with the narrow staircase that lead up to the lumber-room. I found it: now there is an ordinary door there, kept shut. Access to the roof bar is through a new, external staircase, and in front of this door stands a blackboard announcing the day's menu.

I walked through to a large table and sat down. I reckoned that I must be sitting in my old room, Room 8, and, more precisely, somewhere between the bed and the wardrobe. Seeing my balcony doors gone saddened me. But I'd be lying if I said that the atmosphere in the restaurant was unpleasant; it was extremely pleasant, and I had to admit that whoever was responsible for redesigning the place had done so carefully and tastefully.

I was just getting comfortable when a young waitress came up to me and asked how large my party was. When I told her I was alone she moved me to a smaller table nearby, explaining that the large table was booked anyway, and pointed to a card sitting on the tablecloth. Moving tables necessitated a change of room too; I was now in Simos Skouris and Ioanna Chryssovergis's room, the room where I'd been repeatedly subjected to the endless questioning of the former and the arrogant indifference of the latter. From the window the street was partly visible. The waitress reappeared with the menu. I chose the simplest dish available – chicken fillet stuffed with dates in a sweet red wine sauce. Soon more people started arriving, and the place slowly filled up.

'And what will you have to drink with that?' A male voice this time.

'A glass of white, please. And some water,' I added, looking up.

He was wearing a white shirt and tie. I recognised him at once

'Stelios!' I asked in astonishment. 'How are you?'

He didn't say a word. He just stared at me, cold and hostile. He promptly turned and walked off, an aura of loathing in his wake. He returned with two glasses, and filled the empty one with water, pouring all his hatred for me out at the same time. A little later he was back with my order. He put the plate down in front of me, and I thanked him flatly while he maintained his silence. In the meantime I had worked up an appetite, which unlike my sleep, is never vulnerable to stress and upsets.

His hostility came as no surprise. At least it shouldn't have. I was aware of his loyalty to his employer and that there were certain things that he would never be able to forgive me for. I recalled that sinking feeling I'd had about Stelios, right back when I first met him, that he would meet a horrible death. Seeing him again now, so self-assured and so aggressive in his white shirt with just the hint of stomach flab, my instincts told me that those various forms of misfortune would no longer find him attractive, would simply bypass him, and I shouldn't discount the possibility that Stelios might survive well into old age.

I caught the waitress's eye and gestured for the bill. Stelios brought it over. He left it on the table and I was suddenly caught in a very embarrassing dilemma: to tip or not to tip? Being waited on by him was bad enough: knowing how much he hated me, I'm sure that given the choice, he'd much sooner have deposited the chicken on my head than serve it to me on a plate. Now this; the situation could become even more uncomfortable. How do you tip an old acquaintance, particularly one separated from you by a tall wall of loathing? How could it pass itself off as anything other than a slap in the face? On the other hand, it was equally impossible to get up without leaving something, however small, on the saucer. I settled for the latter option: the lesser of two evils.

I went down to the basement. I didn't have any trouble finding the staircase leading from the ground floor into the Internet café. I stopped at the bottom steps and looked around, lost and confused while my stomach tied itself up in knots. The first thing I saw was the bar. A group of about ten young men and women was hanging around there, looking bored and swaying in time to the music. Near the back wall a number of computer terminals had been set up, twenty, maybe more, all occupied. The bluish light lent the place an atmosphere straight out of a sci-fi film until an image of the room flashed across my mind, an image of what it had been like back then. 'Jesus Christ!' I said to myself and turned to leave.

I was intercepted by Stelios, who was standing at the top of the stairs. He'd been watching me. When he realised I'd seen him, he quickly pulled back, but I ran up the stairs after him, grabbed him by the arm and I asked him if we could talk, just for a minute. We stepped out into the garden. He was in no mood to chat and made no effort to conceal the fact.

'I can see that you're not exactly thrilled to see me.'

No answer.

'There are a couple of things I'd like to ask you. First I'd like — '

'I'm busy,' he cut in and tried to walk away.

'Just tell me this,' I said in an attempt to stop him, 'is your master well?'

Your master! I have no idea where that came from, or how it slipped out, but it was too late to take it back. Despite its clumsiness, I think it was a most apt description; besides, he didn't seem to react to it.

'What do you care?'

'I care. Of course I do.'

'After all this time, you suddenly discover that you "care"? Bit late for that, don't you think? A few years too late?'

'I've been abroad. I haven't been around.'

'Yes, yes, I know. You made yourself scarce pretty quickly, didn't you? What you're doing back here now I can't imagine.'

Stelios had grown up; he bore no relation at all to the silly kid I once knew, although the red earring was still faithfully in place.

'Is he well?' I persisted.

'No, he is not well. In four or five years he might be, with a bit of luck,' he said ponderously. I knew what he was trying to say. Of course I did.

'What about the others?'

'Why are you beating about the bush?' Aggressive again. 'Why don't you just come straight out and ask: Where is Halkiolakis? After all, we both know that's who you're interested in. Where is Halkiolakis and what is he doing?

Don't pretend to be concerned about the others.'

He was right, up to a point. I was more interested in Halkiolakis than the others.

'Relax. Halkiolakis has gone home. He's been back on the island for some time now. We haven't seen him since then. See what glad tidings I bring. Now get lost.'

I managed to stop him a second time.

'Aliki?'

He looked at me puzzled.

'Are you short sighted or something? Didn't you see her downstairs?'

With that he vanished.

I hadn't noticed her. I had been so anxious going down those stairs that very little registered at all. I ran back to the Internet café. This time I noticed her immediately. Perched on a barstool, she saw me too, slipped off it and walked across to me. We kissed.

'I saw you earlier, but then you suddenly ran off. Was that because you saw me?'

'I didn't see you.'

This was an unbelievable stroke of luck for me, coming across Aliki like this, although I should perhaps have expected it. There are some places that you never really leave. She asked me what I'd been doing since we last saw each other, and what I was doing with my life. I was hesitant about asking her the same questions, aware of her problems as I was, but she told me without waiting to be asked. She explained that she'd been able to keep the demons at bay for quite some time. That, and her appearance in general, made me think that she was clean, and nothing could have made me happier.

I asked her if she came here a lot. She turned her head (her hair was longer now, and even more beautiful); she motioned to the end of the room, at the back where it was really dark.

'Nothing's changed. I still come here.'

We went on talking for quite some time but with several short pauses; it was like a bad phone connection and you kept getting cut off. Perhaps these pauses coincided with the desire to become more intimate; it was in the air but nothing happened. We parted, promising to get together again soon.

On my way out, I swung round to have a last look at the Aino. Two big motorbikes had stopped outside. Three young men and a woman climbed off them. Her hair was a streaked peroxide yellow.

I turned into the small alleyway. The garden door, the one that led to the reception, was padlocked. The sign with faded letters on it had of course come down. I looked up.

The Aino was sleeping, untouched and invulnerable, high up in its fortress, in the impenetrable fortress of the past.

twenty-three

Nearing the end

We had reached the third and final five-day block of my time at the Aino. After the recent upheavals – the revelation about the secret goddess – I felt that my standing within the sect had changed. I'd pulled back the curtain and entered its sanctuary, which, if it didn't make me the equal of its members, made me equally bound to its pact of silence.

We had become closer through our exchange of secrets. They had given me Aino and that evening on the roof terrace I had laid bare the darkest corner of my life to them. There was no comparison, of course, between the respective worth of each gift. But it is in the nature of gifts that even the most humble present acquires value when given in the right spirit, and in my case nobody could question that aspect of it. There are still times when I wonder how I managed to unburden myself so easily, and wonder if I would ever do so again in the future. I should point out that none of them ever referred to the incident again, or came up to me asking for further explanation or information. My secret was still safely buried. Buried in many more heads than just mine, but buried nonetheless.

The schedule of meetings was followed as usual. I remember the evening I spent with the Skouris-Chryssovergis couple: I was to go and see our actress starring in a production on the opening night and then sit down and talk with the two of them over a meal afterwards. The only drawback for me was that it would involve another late night, but the prospect of getting out of the hotel for an evening at the theatre sounded like fun.

In the taxi on the way down to the theatre, Skouris scaled new heights of pointless chatter. By the time we got out, I had been treated to the plot and every last sub-plot in breathtaking detail, and had been given an exhaustive account of both the sound and lighting design; I knew exactly when the audience was expected to laugh and when the auditorium was likely to fall silent. I was worried that he would keep this up during the performance as well, and in a sense my fears were confirmed. He did manage to stop talking but could not resist squeezing my elbow, my arm, or my knee, every five minutes in an attempt to communicate his enthusiasm for what he was seeing, or else to ensure that I had not missed a certain detail (about which I'd been amply briefed in the car). Then there were his little noises, chuckles, gentle sighs, and '*hhhmmmms*'.

'The Secret Root'. I'd never heard of it or the playwright and can't even remember his name. It was an atmospheric comedy about a strange family living in a provincial town: father, mother, three children and an old man. They lived in a state of constant crisis; everything went wrong all the time as various key pieces of information kept coming to light. These pieces of evidence were literally dug up. According to an ancient family tradition, their ancestors would bury objects and other evidence, so that future generations could find them and communicate with them. The younger ones dug them up, studied their finds, drew conclusions

Stage Set: 'The Secret Root'

which they would share with everybody or else put back for others to discover in the future. Sometimes they buried their own things too, either trying to twist or preserve the truth. Conspiracies were unmasked, oaths of silence broken, incest exposed, children born out of wedlock, their parents proving to be their uncles, their servants relatives, the wealthy abusers, friends enemies, enemies saints, all spinning around a maypole at such a frenzied pace that it was impossible to tell the one person from the next, lies from the truth.

The atmosphere was intense. Even the most hilarious scenes – remember it was a comedy – had something of those old horror movies about it. An enormous, rough-hewn table, monastery benches and endless ancestral portraits made up the scenery.

The actors looked very strange indeed with their wild facial expressions and mud-caked clothes. They made their entrances and their exits through the two doors, one on the left and one on the right. Although I'm no fan of hers, I have to hand it to her – Chryssovergis set herself apart from the rest of the cast. Her transformation was breathtaking. You could almost smell the earth on her breath. She moved very naturally and her voice was coarse – a true peasant. She was brilliant; I was not prepared for it at all. In other words, she was the exact opposite of what she was like in real life: arrogant and pretentious. As I watched, I felt her rise in my estimation and wondered whether perhaps I'd been too hasty in judging her and had underestimated her in the process. These thoughts kept me occupied throughout the first half of the performance.

The interval. We went out to the foyer. Outside, it was raining heavily, and the downpour made it hard to focus on the blow-by-blow account of the author's life Skouris was treating me to. Mercifully, the interval was short and we were soon back in our seats.

The sound of heavy rain then filled the auditorium, this time coming from the loudspeakers. The set was unchanged. Chryssovergis enters from outside. She is soaking wet and clutching a small muddy box which she had just unearthed. She sticks it on the table and with a hammer and chisel tries to prise open the lid. She succeeds and stands there, staring at the contents mutely, before whispering:

'God Almighty!'

She stuffs her hands inside and removes something. At that moment, the most deafening thunderclap reverberates through the entire auditorium, which is duly plunged into darkness.

Everybody, with one exception that is, assumes that this is part of the action. Through the pitch darkness I felt Simos Skouris squeeze my arm as he whispered in my ear:

'What on earth was that?'

'Lightning.'

'There's no lightning in this play,' replied the shaky voice.

The small white emergency lights had come on, and it slowly dawned on me. A few moments of anxious silence followed, as an unpleasant suspicion started to do the rounds of the auditorium, a suspicion that everyone present tried to banish from their minds. Several minutes elapsed and nothing happened. Concern, then the first whispers. By now it was obvious that something was wrong. Then a voice, only slightly louder than the dull murmurs it sought to assert itself over: 'Cut!' Someone in the audience started clapping uncertainly, and another followed suit.

'Now what?' sighed Skouris.

We sat like that for a few more seconds, perhaps as long as a minute, until a shadow eventually came on stage. It was the actor playing the eldest son, holding a lighted candle.

'There has been a power cut,' announced a feint voice. 'A blackout. The entire block has been affected. Please remain seated until power has been restored and the performance will resume immediately.'

We remained seated, but the power showed no signs of coming back on. People started to fidget and some left their seats and tried to get a refund. The performance was called off.

Skouris and I were the last to leave. We waited in the foyer for Chryssovergis, and every so often he'd punctuate the silence with a 'Damned unlucky!'

As the last member of the audience moved away from the theatre, the building, after a nervous jolt, was suddenly flooded with a blinding, unforgiving light, like some spoilt brat sticking its tongue out.

'Damned unlucky!' Skouris repeated, very audibly.

The actors started to file out, back in their own clothes, but still wearing those otherworldly features and expressions. They nodded at us in silent acknowledgement, as though they had all been rehearsing the same gesture, to which Skouris responded with a by now familiar 'Damned unlucky!' Chryssovergis took forever to emerge. When she finally did, it was obvious that she was upset.

'Tonight of all nights! And it was going so well! We've never had such a good first act. Bloody electricity. If we had any sense, we'd be demanding compensation from the power company. Some opening night.'

We ended up in a restaurant somewhere, eating seafood. The atmosphere was tense, and conversation strained. Instead of feeling like their guest, I felt like a fifth wheel. Skouris didn't open his mouth; not that there was anything unusual about that. He was always quiet when she was around. He just sat there, looking at her, waiting for her to be what she was on stage; the leading lady. Nobody would ever guess that this deflated balloon was the same man who had talked a hole in my head only a couple of hours earlier.

Chryssovergis was inexplicably cool towards me, just as she had been during our first meeting. She didn't deign to answer my questions about the play and the production, didn't respond when I complimented her on her acting. The only thing that concerned her, that she gave all her attention to, was how to shell the enormous crabs on the plate in front of her. I couldn't fathom this behaviour as I thought that she had slowly started to warm to me, but now she was treating me with barely-hidden contempt, if not disgust. The explanation came to me only much later, and I'm absolutely convinced that it's the right one: She thought that I had jinxed her opening night and blamed me for her bad luck. She refused to speak to me and avoided eye contact. Needless to say, she did not request any further meetings with me. That night marked the end of what was in any case a most unsuccessful relationship.

I'm sure that Simos Skouris felt very uncomfortable sitting

there, probably all the more so because he knew there was absolutely nothing he could do to break the ice and salvage the situation. And it only got worse.

We stood on the pavement opposite the restaurant waiting for a taxi (we needed two; one to take them home and one to take me back to the hotel). I insisted that they take the first one that drew up, but Skouris, in an attempt to sweeten the bitter pill of a horrific dinner, was adamant that I should have it. I kept telling him that the most sensible thing to do would be for them to go home first, but he wouldn't hear of it. This went on until the taxi driver started to get impatient and Chryssovergis, clearly irritated and anxious to be rid of my unlucky presence, swung round and practically barked at me to get into the taxi.

'Just get in the taxi, Ilias, for God's sake. I don't want to spend the entire night out here!'

I opened the door and sat down in the passenger seat without a word, without protest, without admonishing her for getting my name wrong. The taxi drove off and I watched their figures receding in the wing mirror: the actress had brought her hand up over her mouth, and Skouris was shaking his head.

As for me, I wasn't in the least doubtful that her slip could be traced back to Ilias Alvertos, the guest who'd left his mark on the underside of my wardrobe drawer.

twenty-four

Today I'm going to write about Aliki.

Aliki couldn't remember anything about her parents; they died when she was an infant. Her father worked at the box office of a cinema and her mother worked at the bar inside. They had two children, a boy and a girl. They had been acrobats in their youth, and they died in a train crash. The train was derailed and their wagon pulled them down into a ravine. Ironic, when you think about how they'd spent their best years performing the *salto mortale* and diving into the void. The son, about seven at the time, was put into an orphanage and the little girl, just a year old, was adopted. There was no other family. (I forgot to mention that they were Poles, and if I remember rightly, they also had Russian blood in them. They moved here as soon as their time with the circus came to an end.)

Aliki was raised in a loving environment. Her adoptive parents already had a child, suffering from some sort of muscular disintegrative disorder and died a few years after the adoption. After that, all their love and attention was lavished on Aliki. The couple was comfortably off and denied her nothing.

'They were nice,' she once told me. 'They brought me up

as though I was their own. It was only later they told me I was adopted. They showed me a photograph of my real parents, in their circus outfits, holding my brother before I was born.

They weren't young; I was terrified that I'd lose them too and be orphaned all over again. I reckoned that if I could get to eighteen (that seemed to me to be the cut off point at which you can be orphaned) before they died, I'd be the happiest girl in the world. But it wasn't to be. When I was sixteen my father was diagnosed with cancer and he died within five months. A year later, a few months before my eighteenth birthday, my mother had a heart attack in her sleep. I felt terrible; like all the worrying I'd done had somehow triggered their deaths.'

(I suspect Aliki felt guilty about an awful lot of things, which probably explains how she got mixed up with drugs in the first place.)

After their deaths, she went to live with her brother. I don't know whose idea that was, but I do know that before then, there had been very little contact between brother and sister. They had met only four, perhaps five times in total, but had always made sure that they knew where to find each other.

I haven't mentioned this before: Aliki's brother, the boy who was raised in the orphanage and who later took her in, was Ilias Alvertos, my predecessor at the Aino. He was the reason Aliki turned up one day at the Aino, and he was the reason for all those other visits I had so wildly misinterpreted.

The pieces of the puzzle were slowly falling into place.

She was eighteen, her brother twenty-four. To all intents and purposes, he was a stranger to her: she had no idea what he did for a living, or whether he even had a job. She found herself at his flat one day, pulling a heavy suitcase behind her, with more dolls and cuddly toys in it than clothes.

For most of that first meeting at the restaurant, as she sat there talking to me, her eyes were clouded over. I hung onto her every word. I would have done anyway, even if she'd been reading out the pharmacists' duty roster from the newspaper. I was pleased she was confiding in me; pleased and a bit puzzled. Her words, her expression all made an indelible impression on me.

'I sat down and didn't say anything. Just sat there and looked around. It was a big flat, very light with lots of windows, a new building in an expensive area. He went off somewhere and left me sitting there like that for ages. I could hear some noises, and then he came back and said, "Let me show you your room." He took me by the hand and I asked him what job he did. He didn't answer, he just said, "Don't worry, we won't starve." He talked to me like I was a child; not surprising really, considering how tense and uptight I was. And scared. A new phase in my life was beginning, but I wished he would take me a bit more seriously and treat me like an adult, so I said, "I'll need some sanitary towels. Are there any supermarkets round here?" "Sorry, can't help you there, I'm clean out myself," he said and started laughing. I didn't laugh. I just looked at him. He put his shoes on and we left for the supermarket.'

It was the first time we had talked, Aliki and I. Until then our only contact had been fleeting, those chance encounters and exchanged looks. Now we were sitting opposite each other, all alone in the darkest, most out of the way corner of the restaurant. (The restaurant that's now part of the Alabaster – one of the ones underneath the Aino where I used to have all my meals.) We were alone, talking. Two strangers, two strangers talking for the first time. I was savouring every second of it, although I couldn't understand why she wanted to pour out her entire family history to me. I looked into her eyes, watched the movement of her lips, and listened to her voice.

'He asked me if I had a boyfriend. Before I could answer, he told me that if I wanted to bring boyfriends back to the flat, it was fine by him as long as we didn't make a mess, or play loud music because the neighbours would complain. And his own bed was out of bounds. I told him there was no boyfriend, and asked him if he had a girlfriend. He told me that he did, but he never brought her home. When I asked if I could see a photograph of her, he just snapped, "Fuck the photograph." He paid for the shopping and told me he'd give me a monthly allowance to buy things for the house and to cover my own personal expenses. That was our first day together. Later, on my way to bed, he stopped me, gave me a kiss and said, "I remember you when you were a baby. You cried all the time." Siblings and strangers. I thought how pleased our parents would be if they saw us together again like this.'

She produced a photograph.

'My brother,' she said, putting it down on the table.

Whenever we hear about someone we don't know, we almost inevitably create images of them in our minds; or perhaps the image creates itself – random pieces of information and insignificant details. I don't know why, but hearing and speaking the name Ilias Alvertos brought to mind the image of a fair-haired young man, blue-eyed, well-built, with a very cheerful disposition: a loud voice, fun-loving, perhaps a bit on the ugly side. Everything Aliki had said so far strengthened this impression.

Until I saw the photograph, and realised how wrong I'd been. He didn't look a bit like I'd imagined. Tall, lean, highly-strung, jet-black hair and dark eyes. Extremely attractive.

'Very handsome, isn't he? Unusual looking.'

'Yes, very handsome.'

She smiled and pulled out some more pictures of him

– ten, maybe a dozen.

'I know what you're thinking, but you don't dare say it. You're wondering if I ever fell for him. Well, I'll tell you. I loved being with him, touching his arms, stroking his hair, just looking at him and being proud of him. I admired him a lot. But no. Nothing more than that. Nothing sexual. Not when I knew he was my brother. Not that he didn't create problems for me with men. He did. But it wasn't his fault; they all looked so ugly in comparison. How could I possibly fall in love with a mere mortal when I was living with such a god? Of course I never met the mystery girlfriend. He never mentioned her after that. I'm sure she never existed.'

Something else she said made an impression on me:

'Living with someone as beautiful as that, you can reach saturation point after a while. Their beauty becomes familiar and loses its mythic dimension because it stops being that unreal thing that you only see at the movies or in magazines. You experience it and you get your fill, and then you start to be indifferent to it. It doesn't do anything for you any longer. It was only when I reached that point that I was able to start having relationships with men, even ugly men; I didn't care what they looked like.'

I found a chance to ask about Stelios, if she had been involved with him. She laughed, amazed that I should think such a thing. I mentioned the flowers she used to turn up with, and then disappear into Stelios's room. She shook her head. Obviously there was another explanation.

She carried on talking about her brother, and revealed some very significant things about Ilias Alvertos's life.

When he was sixteen, he ran away from the orphanage, and was found wandering the city streets, high on his new-found freedom. Perhaps instinctively, he ended up in the most dubious parts of town and the most notorious dives. After that, it was only a matter of time: first prostitution, then drugs. Everything happened in a very natural, unforced way. Perhaps the worst thing about it was that he was so comfortable with his choices; his ability to tell good from bad, right from wrong, was severely impaired, if indeed it existed at all. He threw himself into the sewer with an innocent verve, delighted that he could make money so easily, even if it did mean that he had to go to bed with strange men and women every day. When she said that, I couldn't help thinking about Filippos Argyriadis's mother and the ease with which she had allowed herself to sink into the mire; kindred spirits.

By the time he was reunited with his sister, things were rather different. He no longer had to get down and get dirty to maintain a lavish lifestyle: his new patrons were a select few and only took up a few hours of his time every week, sometimes only minutes.

Aliki maintained (I have my doubts) that his kind of life never corrupted her brother, that he remained the same impulsive, innocent child he'd always been, a cheerful little boy who'd jump into a fire to rescue a fellow human being. I had to admit that the face I'd seen in the photo did actually make him come across as more the honest, hard-working ship-hand than the dissolute young man. There was something very carefree about Ilias Alvertos; his entire expression, his smile, they had that lightness of being of someone who has never suspected that life can be such a very complicated business.

'He wasn't corrupt. He was pure gold. Gold remains pure even if you throw it into the filthiest sewer. He never felt guilty about the things he did; in fact he felt very fortunate that so much came to him so easily.'

As I listened to all this, I wondered who this Ilias Alvertos really was: devil in disguise, or an innocent, selfless, naïve angel, sinking in the abyss of his own superficiality?

twenty-five

'And how did you feel when you found out?' I asked Aliki.

'Not too bad, actually. Not too bad. I trusted him, and thought that whatever it was he had done, however extreme, he would never harm himself. It was as though he was under the protection of some guardian angel. Of course there were times when I worried – that's only natural – when he was back late, when he was gone for hours without calling. But to be honest, I never really believed that anything bad would happen to him, nothing that couldn't be sorted out, at any rate. To tell you the truth, I wasn't even that concerned when I found out about the drugs. My love for him clouded my judgement: in my eyes he could do no wrong. Some people, when they're in love, get very anxious and protective; I'm the exact opposite. I wasn't worried at all. It was like I was hypnotised.

He was very tidy too. His clothes, his stuff, everything was very orderly. I never once saw his room in a mess. Everything was always in its place. This forced me to straighten myself out and learn to organise my things. I used to be terrible. The same went for the cleaning. He couldn't stand dirt. What I want to say is this kind of thing inspires confidence, and I was reassured that my brother knew how to take care of himself, just as he took care of me. I never questioned his love for me. I was all he had; he was all I had. I've never understood why he did it.'

'Did what?'

She picked up a paper napkin and started to fiddle with it nervously.

'Never tried to stop me; never did anything to protect me.'

She stopped. I waited. She went on.

'It was my brother who got me into drugs. He got me started.'

I'd suspected as much, sensed that Aliki was on drugs, but never imagined for a minute that her own brother had led her to them.

'I asked him to let me try, and he said yes. He showed me how to recognise the good stuff, what to avoid, and how to use it. The only thing he didn't tell me was where to get hold of it. He said he'd take care of that.'

She was very calm, but her fingers kept nervously folding and unfolding her napkin, over and over again.

'You probably find all of this very shocking,' she said, looking me straight in the eye.

With a spasmodic movement, I shook my head. The truth is that I was beginning to feel uncomfortable. It wasn't so much that I was shocked, like she thought; it was something else. I was suddenly overcome by a strange feeling of inferiority. It was completely irrational. Why on earth should I feel inferior listening to all of this? But I did. When I look back and try to make sense of what I was like back then, I realise that my complex about being from the provinces was still fairly acute; I was the country bumpkin who'd come to the big city to get an education, and whenever I heard about things, even potentially deadly habits like drug-taking, things that were so alien to the world I came from, it felt like a development had somehow taken place in me. Drugs and prostitution in some sense struck me as hopelessly exotic. What could I possible share with her from my own experience that could begin to match that? The only thing I could offer was my grave, unsmiling face, so I sat just and listened to her with obvious seriousness.

'Of course he would never have let me turn tricks to get the money. He'd never have allowed anything like that. Not that I would have been able to bring myself to do it. He could. It didn't bother him. But me, no. Never.'

She talked at length about life with her brother. About the junkies, about the incredible highs she'd had. At one point I managed to work out how old she was when she started all this: only seventeen or eighteen. And then it was as if I was jolted awake from a deep sleep, which till then had made me immune to everything I'd heard, and I was overcome by feelings of disgust for the bastard who'd so casually got his own sister into drugs.

'Don't you see?' I said, choked with outrage, 'Don't you see what a sick mind he's got? Whatever it is that he feels for you, it certainly isn't love.'

She looked at me in astonishment and just sat there clutching the origami flower she'd folded out of the napkin.

'I thought you'd realised,' she said. 'My brother's dead.'

twenty-six

'Dead!' The word echoed for a second time inside my head. It had not once crossed my mind that the person we had been talking about all this time was dead. It's true that she talked about him in the past tense, but that doesn't necessarily mean anything.

The news certainly took me aback, but I was far from shocked by it. That way of life is precarious. It might sound harsh, even evil, but I felt a surge of satisfaction at the news. Ilias Alvertos was doomed: he had taken his little sister into his care and instead of protecting her, had ruined her. No matter how good-looking he was, he could never make up for that. A lost soul, as I said before. Naturally, I didn't share these insights with Aliki.

'I'm so sorry,' I whispered.

She looked more worried than sad. She was trying to sort out whatever it was she wanted to say next. Whatever it was that was weighing so heavily on her. Whatever it was that had made her ask to see me.

As I said before, we had met at the restaurant downstairs from the hotel, on the main road. It was late, around 11.30 pm, two days before my stay at the Aino was due to come to an end. Earlier on I had been at another meeting with the director. He wanted us to discuss three possible endings to the film script he was working on. It was very tiring – he insisted on a thorough analysis and rationale for everything I said, down to the last throwaway comment. Perhaps it was just cumulative tiredness; there was nothing I wanted more than to have something to eat and go to bed. I ordered, finished my meal quickly and had just stood up to leave when I saw Aliki standing there in front of me, rather like in the cinema when an unexpected appearance is instantly captured in the very next frame. She looked straight at me, terrified and embarrassed. It was then that I heard her voice for the first time. She asked if we could talk. I decided it would be better to change tables as mine was right by the entrance. We picked a table in an alcove at the back of the restaurant. The alcove was like a room apart. It was a horrible, mossy green colour, unlike the rest of the restaurant, which was freshly painted, bright and airy. Through the tiny square window in it, you could see the flaking bark of tree, half concealed by a filthy green curtain, uncertainly suspended from a yellowing wire. If I hadn't been so tired, I would have been totally stunned by Aliki's sudden appearance, and the entire air of conspiracy surrounding it. But exhaustion can cancel out almost anything.

We ordered a bottle of red wine, and she told me that she'd been looking for a chance to talk to me for some time now. She was clearly uncomfortable so in an attempt to get the conversation going, I asked if she was related to the collector or any of the others. She shook her head, and started talking about her parents (the circus, the train crash etc.). We then moved on to her brother (everything I dealt with a few pages back) until we got to the point where she told me that he was dead. All this took up a good hour. With a slightly comic gesture, she offered me her origami flower, and I couldn't help noticing how masculine her fingers were.

It was then that I confessed that I knew her brother's name. Her surprise grew as she listened to the whole story about the drawer in my wardrobe, and what I found written underneath it. She had a hard time believing it, and might even have questioned my grip on reality, so I offered to take her upstairs so she could see it for herself.

We went up separately to avoid any unwanted attention. While I waited for her, I quickly emptied the drawer because I was far too bashful to take out my underwear in front of her. I turned it over and froze. There was nothing underneath. Not a single mark. I shuddered and pulled out the other three drawers, just in case I had put them back in the wrong order. No – just as I thought. It had vanished without trace. I inspected the first drawer again, and noticed that the bottom surface looked lighter than the wood on the sides, newer somehow. Someone had obviously been at it with sandpaper. As fast as lightning follows thunder, the image of Tina Paraschis hanging onto the edge of the boat we took out to that decommissioned ship flashed across my mind. I'll never forget how worried she looked when she asked me I how I knew Ilias Alvertos, and the immeasurable relief on her face when I explained the whole business with the drawer. Then I recalled the utter desperation of Ioanna Chryssovergis as soon as she realised that she had called me Ilias by mistake that mad night at the theatre.

There was obviously a deep connection there, deep and dark, and one I knew nothing about. Perhaps now was the time – I thought – that I would find out all about it, from the man's own sister.

My disappointment must have been written across my face. Aliki worked out what had happened as soon as she opened the door. I showed her the drawer and explained. She didn't have any difficulty believing what I told her. When I scribbled an approximation of Ilias Alvertos's signature on a piece of paper, as best as I could remember it from underneath the drawer, her eyes were shot through with a shiny silver spark. It seemed that I had done quite a good job.

'Yes,' she whispered (our entire communication was conducted in a whisper in case someone was eavesdropping outside). 'He liked leaving traces of himself wherever he went, always in secret, hidden places. It was a game he liked to play…'

She asked me what else I had seen scored into the drawer. I told her exactly what it said, the table with the dates and his meetings with the group. I also told her that the 15th November, when the group meeting had been scheduled, was the last date to be filled in; the rest were blank, as though the curtain had come down before the end of the final act.

When I said this, Aliki leapt up from the bed where she had been sitting holding the drawer with the destroyed evidence, threw herself onto the door and glued her eye to the keyhole. She stood there like that for a number of minutes, surveying the corridor and then turned round and came up to me so close that I was pinioned against the wall. She looked at me intently; I found it hard to interpret what her look meant, but she held me prisoner like that for a while until she leant over and whispered in my ear:

'You've got to get out of here. Now.'

'I've only got two days left,' I answered, 'I'll be gone in two days.'

She backed off but was soon on top of me again. She brought her mouth back up to my ear, and in a barely audible breath said:

'If they request a group meeting, don't go, whatever you do.'

Without realising it, my voice had suddenly got louder but I was able to return it to a suitable volume almost immediately.

'I've already attended one. Really. It was a very special day for me, honestly.'

'Did you all go down to the basement?'

'Basement? No, we went up to the roof terrace. Why? Is there a basement?'

I knew there was a basement; what I really meant to ask her was 'Is the basement in use?'

She looked around, uncomfortably.

'I'd better not hang around here. Perhaps it was a mistake coming to find you. I'll leave.'

She pushed the door ajar, made sure the coast was clear, and skipped out noiselessly.

It was close to two. What had been an extremely tiring day was ending on an unexpectedly emotional note. Shattered, I flopped down onto the bed. I didn't have the strength even to go over everything that had happened in my mind, everything that had been said, everything that had been revealed, everything I felt. Sleep came and carried me off in an instant; I didn't even have enough time to get undressed.

I slept, but it did nothing to refresh me as my mind was still active even though my body had shut down. The image of Ilias Alvertos, the real Ilias Alvertos, flickered on and off, against an incomprehensible background of iron shafts stuck into the sand, looking with an alternately cold and beseeching look in his eyes; sometimes filled with tears and other secretions, sometimes dry as dust. He spoke to me; I spoke to him, but I cannot remember anything from this disjointed conversation, nothing at all – except this one phrase: one of my own phrases which I shouted at him repeatedly:

'*The metal men got you! The metal men got you! The metal men killed you!*'

I've no idea where this had come from, this madness with the metal men, but I had the unshakeable certainty that by it

I meant the five links in the chain, nothing else. It was such a vivid feeling that I woke up in a panic.

'*The metal men killed you.*'

My heart was racing out of control. That's why Aliki wanted to see me! To protect me. That's what she wanted to say. The metal men had killed her brother and now it was my turn. She was warning me. 'You've got to get out of here. Now.' Her precise words. My life was in danger. I was in danger!

As the seconds ticked along, I became gradually more alert and this idea seemed increasingly absurd to me. I might not have known them for long, that was true, but these people were the most unlikely murderers. Only the most disturbed mind could imagine them plotting my death. My heartbeat had relaxed and I was once again in possession of my senses.

My eyes, rounded in the darkness, had settled on the cupboard standing across the room from my bed. The drawer Ilias Alvertos had written on had not been replaced and the pitch-black gap it left in the lower section of the wardrobe stood out against the darkness of the room. Sleep was creeping up on me again, even though my eyes were wide open. I imagined (or did I dream it?) that I got out of bed and curled up inside that pitch-black gap, slid down a shaft, and found myself almost immediately in the basement. But no image of the basement was supplied. Just darkness. Darkness and nothing else.

twenty-seven

As soon as I got out of bed the next morning, I realised that I had completely recovered from my nightmare. As my tiredness wore off, it took with it all those thoughts and outlandish fears, even the slight hangover a bad dream can leave you with. All that remained was the sweet aftertaste of my meeting with Aliki, and the image of her face lingering in my mind.

'Just one more day after this,' I whispered to myself and started to dress in preparation for my meeting with the collector.

I was looking forward to it, was even happy at the thought of seeing him. I respected and admired him, and with my ordeal coming to an end, I could even say that I admired him unreservedly. To me he was like a multicoloured bird (I say this even though he despised birds), with cold, phosphorescent streaks, a long beak and a shrill voice. Beautiful, wise and aloof. I imagine this bird locked up in that cage I'd seen in the garden, pacing its confines deep in thought, hanging from the wires, poking its large beak through the bars at me in a threatening but basically harmless display. I proceeded to place the rest of the sect inside the cage: a round pink goldfinch – the actress, fluttering around and pecking randomly at the seeds at the bottom of the cage. Right behind her stands Skouris, the colourless quail, who does everything he can to distract himself and the others from the fact that there isn't the slightest hint of colour in his plumage. He stands there, dully swelling up and deflating again. As for Argentina Paraschis, our photographer, I'll make her a turtle-dove. Her fine, rather sharp features admirably suit the bird's delicate nature. I remember seeing one as a boy. They're a slightly reddish colour, a colour that suits her. Halkiolakis last. 'Halkiolakis', the perfect name for a species of bird: 'Halkiolakis migratorius': medium-sized, with a bright yellow chest and throat, thick black bill, skulking at a distance from the others, perched on his steely blue legs, his wings shimmering in the sunlight, he surveys everything around him.

And after creating them, one by one, I sit back and admire my work. I think about F and his aquarium, and with what care he selected all his fish in an attempt to get the balance of colour inside the water just right. I did the same with my birds. The overall picture I created, as it is now fixed it in my imagination, is very pleasing indeed. The different shades, the shapes, the behaviours, everything hangs together beautifully.

(I admit that it wasn't then – while I was getting dressed for my appointment with Argyriadis – that I dreamt up all these details. Some of them I made up as I went along. I admit it – for the record – just to make sure that the integrity of this record is not compromised. I get carried away sometimes; an overactive imagination is, it seems, an incurable disease.)

What was bearing heavily on my mind before I even knocked on his door was how I could broach the subject of Amo again. My time was coming to an end and I desperately wanted him to show me the codex. Not because I had any doubts that it existed; well, not exactly. It was the fact that I knew that only by holding the codex in my hands, only by touching it, would I be able to satisfy this burning curiosity.

Argyriadis, however, after watching me struggle to come out with the question, did not respond positively, but neither did he seem to be trying to renege on his original promise.

'You are bursting with anticipation. I can understand that. But I won't allow either of us to act unadvisedly. You give me the impression that you fail to approach certain things with the necessary *gravitas*, and in your enthusiasm, you are prepared to risk everything. I can't blame you for that, but I am determined to keep a tight rein on the situation. How long have you known about the existence of the goddess? Not even a week? And you have already started demanding to see the evidence. It doesn't bother me, believe me; neither your ambition nor your brazenness disturb me. I consider them to be among the most charming of human imperfections, especially in the young, but the point is that I have a duty to protect you. Pay heed: it will take a long time before I can be persuaded to hand over the keys to you. Watch out, the way you're going, you're bound to get into trouble.'

I understood; if I crossed her, the goddess would exact revenge.

The contradictions in that man! I found him baffling. One minute he came across as a cold pragmatist, the next he would lose his nerve like the superstitious old women back home. I was in no doubt: it was sheer cowardice that had kept him from revealing the secret of Aino all these years.

I made it as clear to him as I could that I didn't deserve to be given anything; all I wanted was to be allowed to take a look at the codex, nothing else, although I did add that I respected the way he wished to handle the matter and would always be grateful for the confidence he had shown in me.

'Oh. You want to look at the codex? Nothing else?' He was quiet for a few moments. 'And when would you like to do that?'

'There's no time like the present!' I shouted and listened as my voice echoed like a Native American call.

'What? Do you imagine that I carry that priceless manuscript around with me? Or keep it lying around in a drawer?' (He amplified this comment by pulling open and slamming shut his desk drawer.) 'Ready to be pulled out and shown to anyone who expresses an interest? What you ask of me will put me to a great deal of trouble. But you are trouble anyway. A lot of trouble. I will give in to the vehemence of your request; I always make a point of trying to keep my guests happy. But you'll have to be patient for a few days. Wait!' (Something had occurred to him.) 'Perhaps I can speed up the process after all. Come and find me tonight. Make it late though. After midnight.'

And then he got rid of me.

The same day, I was seen by the rest of them, as planned, individually, at four different places. I can't remember a thing about those meetings.

After midnight, as ordered, I knocked on the collector's door. He told me to sit down. I moved the heavy hurricane lamp and sat down numbly. He then positioned a reading lamp, its bulb just the right strength, on top of the enormous pile of books next to me.

Quite unceremoniously, he placed a hard, flat box on my lap.

'Open it,' he ordered.

I removed the lid and slowly lifted out the ancient manuscript, with the same amount of care as if I were picking up a wounded bird. Half in a trance, I turned the first page. The parchment rustled under my trembling fingers. My eyes leapt from line to line, moving down through the rows of curlicued writing, line by line, irregularly, blindly, without retaining any meaning or information as they went. They'd stumble occasionally on certain words that jumped off the page like loose stones – the most frequent one was 'Aino', then they'd rest a while before setting off again on their thorn-strewn path in tears. The collector had to keep wiping my face; my eyes were streaming.

'We don't want those salt drops falling onto the parchment now, do we?'

I had looked through the entire thing. The text concluded on a single pen stroke, an arabesque bearing the name of the scribe in code, etched with enormous care. An indecipherable signature. I started to flick through the pages again from the beginning, more slowly, more analytically. This time I was able to digest some things, complete phrases, and understand the meanings of words – or at least make an educated guess about them. The weak little bird in my hand had stopped trembling.

Argyriadis stood guard next to me all this time: I felt a sudden urge rise in me, an unseen muscular spasm which, if left unchecked, would have made me jump up like a spring, push the collector out of my way, and start running. Running and running, running fast and tirelessly, as far away from the hotel as I could get, clutching Aino tightly to my chest, stopping only when we were safe. If only I could. If only I had the guts to make off with it, and disappear without trace.

I looked up; my eyes met his. I'm quite sure he could read my mind. I winced as he put his hand on my shoulder, his long fingers reaching the nape of my neck. He applied a small amount of pressure there, to some hidden spot he was only too familiar with. And with one touch he had paralysed my will, paralysed my mind. With his other hand he nimbly extracted the codex from my grasp. The box snapped shut and disappeared into the dark recesses of one of his desk drawers.

Neither of us was in a hurry to break the silence. The wind outside was all that could be heard, accompanied by the creaking metal of the cockerel weather vane.

'Make a note of today's date,' he said after a long interval. 'Remember that today was the day that you witnessed a divine revelation. You might never have believed what I told you otherwise. And you'd be right. What value, after all, do words have? It is necessary to feel it between your fingers, to touch it for yourself, the thing itself. Today you came face to face with Aino for the first time.'

I did precisely as he said. I made a note of the date: Saturday, 4th May 1991.

twenty-eight

My last day.

I'm confident that I have managed to recall the events of the last day with great accuracy. Suppose someone asked me to reproduce everything that happened, I'm sure I could repeat everything I said as well as what the others said, word for word, complete with body language, gestures and facial expressions.

I'm convinced of it, but at the same time I also acknowledge that the opposite might be true: that I might be mistaken. I frequently am. For example, when I watch an old film again after many years, the thing that strikes me is that there are certain scenes that I play over in my mind again and again, scenes that I swear I could describe in the most minute detail. When I see the film again, as I wait impatiently for my favourite scene to come, the scene that I have kept so hidden in the deepest recesses of my mind, I notice entire sequences that are totally unfamiliar to me. It finally comes, and what do I see? Everything is different. The man in the waterproof is not wearing glasses, and he's not standing in front of the car; he's sitting in the passenger seat, and he's got the beginnings of a beard. Dark brown hair, not blonde. And so on. I could give you hundreds more examples.

So I ask myself, just how faithfully am I reproducing reality when I say that I have perfect recall of a situation or of a conversation? Only if someone had filmed the actual events for me to compare my recollections with, would I be able to answer that question. I'm sure I'd be stunned by the differences and at the mechanisms of distortion: distortion on the one hand, lacunae on the other. Unfortunately, memories too carry with them the marks of human imperfection. I'm beginning to believe that truth itself changes and what we remember happening gradually distances itself from what actually happened.

I woke up late, at my leisure; there were no meetings scheduled for the morning. There was nothing on until the evening when we were all due to get together for my farewell dinner, which, weather permitting, would be held on the roof terrace.

Still lying in bed, luxuriating in the softness of my enormous pillow, I was enveloped by a sense of profound satisfaction. Time flowed like water, and though I had the impression that my days at the hotel had flown past, it also seemed that time had expanded to fit both the major and minor incidents that had occurred. I was grateful that I'd had the chance to experience something of this kind.

I was tempted to spend the whole day in bed. I wanted to be alone, not talk to anyone, clear out my head from all those interminable discussions, all those contacts, the effort of it all. Just lie there, my head void of everything, my mouth closed, my powers of perception deactivated. At about 3 pm hunger took me downstairs to the restaurant. On my way out I took a look through the window in the corridor and spotted Aliki coming in carrying her customary bunch of flowers, this time dazzling white carnations. I wondered what it was that brought her here so often – whatever the attraction was, it wasn't me – and carrying flowers to boot. (This was something she had never explained, not even that evening we spent together in the restaurant, and curiosity had been eating me up ever since: what was her connection to the Aino? I had not yet managed to ask her.)

I toyed with the idea of following her, to see where she was going. I sped down the staircase and sat down in the small sofa in the reception area. A few seconds later, I heard voices. She was with Stelios who was sweeping the corridor outside. They walked inside together, exchanged a few words while I followed them in the large mirror in the entrance hall. He went back outside to finish up, and she went into his room. I could hear the scratching of Stelios's wire broom outside and concluded that the slow, tired pace he was sweeping at indicated that Aliki was not waiting for him, and that he wasn't worried about leaving her alone in his room.

Then it occurred to me that she might be visiting his father for some reason. I walked up to the door, stood right outside but couldn't hear a thing, not the slightest whisper.

I knocked discreetly. In the unlikely event that the father opened the door, I would find some kind of excuse, but what if Aliki herself opened? Quite simply: I would ask her if we could talk. But nobody opened the door. I knocked again, harder. Nothing.

'Alright,' I thought, 'It wouldn't exactly be breaking the law if I opened the door.'

I wanted to get out of sight before Stelios came back, so I turned the handle and walked in. There was nobody there.

'Aliki!' I said in a low steady voice.

Nothing. I took a look around, carefully. Nobody there at all, and the window was closed from the inside. There was no other way out. I thought that perhaps I had been misled by the reflection in the big mirror and that she hadn't come in here at all and instead had gone through some other, secret doorway. I went back out in to the hall and checked, and was not surprised to find nothing. No, there was no other door. Aliki had gone into Stelios's room and that was that. Unless my eyes had suddenly started playing tricks on me. I went back inside and called her name once more, louder this time. Once more I had absolutely no response.

I crouched down and looked under the bed. Nothing hidden there. No Aliki. There weren't an awful lot of choices of hiding place in the room: a couple of beds, a metal desk and the large wardrobe.

I was standing in front of the wardrobe and noticed that the decorative carving running along the top was almost identical to the pattern on the one in my room. Obviously the work of the same carpenter. I pictured Aliki hiding behind one of its five doors, for a reason I could not understand, holding her breath, desperately waiting for me to get out of the room. I imagined myself opening the doors one by one, searching for her behind the racks of hanging clothes and folded blankets until I eventually found her, hunched up between the shirts and the winter coats, scared out of her wits as I asked her why she was avoiding me and what she was trying to hide.

'She might even be watching me now,' I thought, 'through some crack or keyhole.'

This suspicion only heightened my sense of excitement. First I opened the single door, which revealed a series of shelves full of tools, organised very neatly. I moved on to the double door in the middle; Stelios's stuff. I could smell Stelios in there but not Aliki.

'Aliki!' I said decisively as I pulled open the twin doors of the last section of the wardrobe: Stelios's father's jackets, hanging regimentally, and a bunch of coat hangers pushed to the other side, leaving a gap. Where I expected to see the back panel of the cupboard I found myself staring into a big black hole. That monstrous wardrobe had been concealing a doorway!

I climbed inside, in between the clothes. To steady myself, I held onto the horizontal rail just like all the hooks of the clothes hangers. I stretched out my leg in front of me to get a feel of the large hole, much as one would dip a toe into the sea. I was on firm ground, but I realised that the sole of my foot was being raised up by a step, which made me twice as cautious.

(I might be describing all this in a cold, detached way; at least that's what it feels like as I read through these lines, and perhaps risk losing the fact that all the while I felt something between profound awe and horror.)

My eyes had trouble adjusting to this near darkness, but my sense of touch told me that there was a staircase in front of me, one that went down, presumably to the basement.

I stretched out my right hand to the side, but however far I reached, I never hit anything and was just grasping at the void. On the other side, however, to my left, I did hit a wall, and although the staircase was quite broad, I'd managed to fall onto the wall with all my weight, which with its hard surface kept me from falling.

As my eyes slowly adjusted to the dim light (the reflection of another light somewhere) my legs became more confident. Halfway down the stairs, the room started to come into view on my right, in a blur at first, until I reached the end of that endless flight of stairs.

I found myself inside an enormous living room. Bizarre. The last thing you'd expect to find in a basement of a seedy hotel. It was a pretty ordinary sitting room, one that would not be at all out of place as a reception room in a fairly wealthy home. Nice big comfortable sofas, various armchairs, antique dressers with ornate carvings on them, as well as a selection of small, ornate tables, desks and bureaux. A glass cabinet holding the china, and another holding the silver. A piano. Heavily framed paintings, crystal chandeliers, a wall clock, accurate to the minute. Plant stands occupied a couple of corners, as well as clay statues, of that kind which in the past used to adorn the facades of mansions. One was a vulture, the other a Tanagra statuette.

The light was coming from further inside, where, if I was not mistaken, Aliki was (why she was there was still a mystery). But I couldn't see that far in and anyway, the basement consisted of different areas, and was not just one single space. You had to turn off the sitting room further down and then turn again, making up a 'Π' sign. I walked slowly, my footfall absorbed in the plush of the heavy carpeting. I wasn't in any particular hurry; my initial anxiety to track down Aliki had evaporated, and all I wanted to do now was to explore this mysterious basement. I looked up, down, left and right, rather like you would in a museum. I didn't touch anything; I was sure that it was inhabited, that if I opened the drawers I would find evidence of occupation: nail clippers, paperclips, and in the desks, documents, notes, bills. There wasn't a speck of dust to be seen. Stelios and his father – I was sure the cleaners never came down here – they maintained very high standards of housekeeping here in this hermetic dominion.

If I had to guess the length of the long wall of the sitting room, I'd say it was about twenty-five metres. At the end of that long wall opposite you could see a collection of portraits, male and female. All the sitters were accompanied by some kind of animal: cat, dog, horse, even a goose. At the point where the right-hand wall came to an end, there was an opening, without a door, leading to the second room, a spacious bedroom.

In the middle of it stood a regal-looking bed, made up

in luxury linens. But what really caught my eye in there was the wooden sculpture nailed high up onto the wall. It was a female head, leaning slightly forward, with just a hint of cleavage visible. Looking at it up close, it looked like decaying driftwood, or perhaps an old figurehead. Above it, only a few centimetres from the ceiling, I noticed a tiny little window. I was sure that it was the one I'd seen from the garden, the one that was concealed behind the ivy. The pane was painted over in opaque paint.

So far there had been just enough light to help me along, and that light came from in here: next to the bed was a standard lamp; it was on.

On the wall to my right was another doorway, closed off by a heavy curtain. I was just about to pull it back when I heard voices. Clear voices. I was able to pick out Aliki's; she was speaking softly, somewhat breathlessly. There were silences in between and the talking resumed. I couldn't work out what she was saying with any precision, just the odd

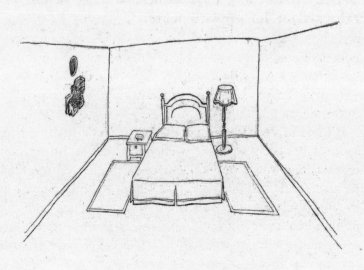

The basement: the room with the bed

word and phrase: 'bound', 'wings', 'eyelids', 'sharper at first', things which made little sense on their own and even less in combination. I never did pick up a second voice answering her though.

Without pulling back the curtain, which stretched like a solid panel right down to the floor, I stood there eavesdropping for some time without moving. I knew she was somewhere very close and that we were separated only by a piece of cloth. Through a tiny gap in the side I could see that it was dark on the other side, so I wouldn't be able to slip in unnoticed because the light from the bedroom would give me away the moment I pulled back the curtain.

As the minutes went by, the more I was sure that what I was hearing, the random phrases and expressions, were not part of a conversation but various threads of a monologue. When there was no longer any doubt in my mind that Aliki was in fact talking to herself in there, I threw back the curtain and ventured into the third room.

That's it for now. I'll stop here. Writing all this has exhausted me. Tomorrow. Tomorrow.

twenty-nine

The muttering stopped instantly. I couldn't hear any breathing – not my own, not anybody else's. I couldn't see anything, but I was sure that I was visible, in the way that you're visible when you try to get into the cinema late. You are blind, but everybody else is equipped with twenty-twenty vision, looks you up and down, sniggering about your temporary disability which causes you to trip and stumble endlessly. I was a bit embarrassed at first, waiting for my eyes to be at less of a disadvantage. Darkness and silence. My cheeks were cool. Cool damp air. I sensed that the room was quite big, a cellar maybe, with the pervasive smell of something sweet and rotten.

It was then that I noticed the flame, right at the back. Candlelight. I walked towards it, got nearer, and heard someone moving. I heard the light rustle from the clothes of another human being. Her dress was getting whiter, a little further ahead. I could see much more clearly now. She had moved away from the candle and I could make out her arms, wrapped defensively around her body; I heard her breathing, saw her eyes gleaming in the darkness, looking at me…

'Aliki?'

Out of the blue, she leapt on me, squeezing me so tightly

in a desperate embrace. Our faces touched.

'What are you doing here?' she whispered into my hair.

'I followed you.'

'What do you want?'

'To talk.'

For a brief moment, our lips came together.

'What do you want to know?'

'What is this place? You told me not to come down here, remember?'

'Not with them.'

'What is this place?' I repeated.

She relaxed her grip on me and we looked at each other.

'Nobody lives here. Nobody ever comes here anymore, except me.'

It suddenly occurred to me that there might be a second person hiding somewhere in the darkness. It was as though she could read my thoughts.

'I always come here alone.'

I turned towards the candle. I left Aliki and walked over to the flame and was able to see everything, absolutely everything: the flame illuminated a small mound; the word grave immediately suggested itself. A hill of flowers. The ones at the bottom had turned black and had withered. The higher up you looked, the more stages of decomposition you could see: a rotten red, rotten pink, mouldy green and so on, mouldy pomegranate – all adorned by this morning's bright white carnations.

I knew at once what I was looking at. No explanation was needed. I'd known since that dream, the one that made me cry out loud: '*The metal men got you! The metal men got you! The metal men killed you!*' I had refused to take it seriously at the time, my waking logic demanded that I dismiss the possibility and banish the information that had found its way into my subconscious. It was impossible to ignore it any longer. I knew. I knew that the guest had been killed and was buried right there. I knew who had killed him. I knew everything.

Aliki simply confirmed it.

'Sometimes they can be quite terrifying. It's not their fault; things just happen all of a sudden and I know exactly what happened in my brother's case, and that's what really important. I wouldn't have been able to stand not knowing; that would have been too hard.'

She explained that the group kept records of all their guests, detailed records. These records contained not only details of what emerged in meetings but also opinions, comments and deliberations – everything they wanted to know, aspects they needed to study and how to surround the person in question; how to set the trap. And of course all their conclusions. They wrote everything down, distilled the essence of each guest and preserved it forever in their ledgers. The ultimate object of the exercise was to build up over time what I could only describe as a 'human library', each volume in it would contain the same material, the texture, the blood of real, living human beings. A select few; the carefully handpicked guests. A unique treasure. That was their aim.

Aliki had access to their confidential archive.

'It was only through reading it that I really got to know my brother, by reading their notes. I didn't read them just once. I read them several times. There are entire passages that I could reel off to you without making a single mistake. It's not that I found out things I didn't know before, that's not what I mean. I just discovered a different way of reading him; that's what changed. And I learnt to love him more. And I owe that to those five people.'

'The five people who killed him?' I shouted, unable to keep my voice in check. 'How can you bring yourself to come down here? How can you stand seeing them? How come you don't hate them?'

'My brother's death was an accident. It was one of those moments when things just get out of control. One false step. Could happen to anyone.'

I explained that the word 'accident' filled me with scepticism. She let it go but it was obvious that she needed to believe in them. Aliki wanted to talk about everything in turn, starting with how her brother got involved with the five. (Or four as they then were, before Skouris joined.)

Alvertos had been Halkiolakis's discovery. He had spotted him at some cheap dive, the escort of an older, very well known actor the director had once worked with. He was immediately struck by how handsome the young man was, and asked who he was. The actor, very protective of his new acquisition, refused to tell him. Undeterred, Halkiolakis found a way to meet him without the actor's help and right away invited him to the Aino as a guest on their 'orientation and study' programme. Attached to the invitation was a generous sum of money to compensate him for his time (more than three times the amount I received). Alvertos agreed to make himself available from the beginning of the following month and on 8th November 1986 he walked into the Aino, and checked in for a twelve-day stay.

Whether Ilias Alvertos was endowed with gifts other than that of beauty, I am not in a position to say. But I do know that it was his beauty and not some intellectual quality that prompted the invitation and the entire programme had been devised as an investigation into beauty: the endurance of beauty, the distortion of beauty, the idea of beauty. The sect had found the perfect research subject, the very embodiment of the ideal.

In the notes they kept, Aliki read about how thrilled they all were with him. He wasn't only handsome, he was clever, and very accommodating. He was a pleasure to work with, and they had no difficulty explaining the subject of their enquiry on each occasion; they would discuss it with him and they even let him in on their conclusions. He would listen, understand and participate. He had no reservations. If asked, he wouldn't hesitate to take off his clothes and sit there stark naked for the duration of the meeting; or smile, lie down, allow a finger inside his mouth, a finger wanting to explore his teeth; or be kissed, anything, if it helped. The most amazing thing of all though was that none of it bothered him at all, on the contrary, it amused him, and he always performed to the best of his ability.

A clear example of their enthusiasm for Ilias: he mentioned that his favourite animals were birds, especially birds of prey. The very next morning, a cage with a dark grey hawk pacing up and down inside it appeared in the back garden. When he saw it, Alvertos could barely contain his joy, and was so moved that tears rolled down his cheeks. He enfolded all four of them in his arms and smothered them with kisses. They agreed that as soon as the prescribed twelve days were over, they'd take a trip up to the mountains together and ceremonially release the hawk. Of course they never did.

It is more than certain that this move, the amazing surprise-present, won the heart of their charming guest. And it was all the more meaningful for the fact that Filippos Argyriadis had a natural aversion to birds. The young man spent hours watching the wild bird up close and experienced the most delightful, perhaps, caper of his life, and at the same time overflowed with gratitude.

Till then, the sect always conducted its meetings with its guests in that huge room in the basement, and it's not impossible that the room had been specially designed for the purpose. It was there, in the basement, where Ilias Alvertos's final scene was played out. Of course I refer to the group

173

meeting he attended on the 15th November, the last time a meeting was held down there.

Everything went ahead quietly and smoothly, as things tend to before they go badly wrong. After a few minutes of casual conversation in the sitting room Filippos Argyriadis stood up to speak:

'Wonderful! Let's do something a bit different today.' The others instantly got to their feet.

They asked Alvertos to undress. He did. Someone then suggested they adjourn to the bedroom. The young man stretched out on the bed, awaiting instructions. He had complete confidence in their motives and in what they were planning to do to him. They tied his limbs to the posts of the bed using brightly coloured strips of silk, and gave their word that his 'ordeal' (their word) would be over as quickly as possible.

He looked at them in calm expectation.

'We should all be here today,' said one of them, possibly the actress.

The special, rather sensitive subject that they wanted to explore was this: the fragility of beauty and its vulnerability to pain, to fear and to the sense of exclusion. They were interested in the endurance of the sweet lines of this exquisite face when the body is subjected to intolerable suffering, is gasping for breath, racked with pain and brought to the limits of agony.

I think it's important to stress at this point that there was no evidence of sadistic enjoyment in the conduct of the experiment. Causing pain to Alvertos caused them embarrassment and distress, not pleasure. The director performed the unenviable task. It's interesting that nowhere in their notes do they furnish details on what methods and procedures were used. Only the subject's reactions and comments made about his reactions were noted. They were recorded in extraordinary detail, along with the stages, the intensity and the resulting level of distortion.

Aliki obviously couldn't tell me word for word what she'd read, especially not about that particular moment. Neither could she explain the precise nature of the experiment in any more detail. I only remember that she said – and this could well be a basic conclusion – pain does not destroy beauty, rather it elevates it, bringing to it the dimensions of greatness and holiness.

'My brother's death was an accident,' she repeated.

I could see that Aliki believed that and always would believe it. Maybe I do too. Ilias Alvertos's death might have been an accident.

This difficult meeting was drawing to a close, the subject's responses to pain had been studied, and recorded, and Tina Paraschis kept a photographic record for posterity. The only thing that had proved impossible was to provoke fear in their guest. Perhaps his personality explained that, the variety of his experiences. Certainly the unshakeable trust he felt in the hands of his friends rendered all attempts to frighten him unsuccessful. They had given up hope of witnessing beauty reacting with fear when Halkiolakis suddenly came up with the bright idea of releasing one of the subject's ankles, and moving the silk binding from his feet to his neck, whispering in a menacing tone:

'What if I told you that what we wanted all along was to see your beautiful form expire? That what we wanted all along was to witness the final showdown between two titans: beauty and death, to see who'd prevail? What would you say to that?'

Alvertos didn't move. He just looked at him and smiled, not believing a word of it, even though Halkiolakis was jerking the silk tighter and tighter. Halkiolakis never thought to stop. Not even when a strong spasm caused Alvertos's free foot to flail up into the air, did it occur to him to relax his hold, not even when the collector ordered him to stop, not even the entreaties of the two women could stop him pulling it tauter and tauter. He didn't listen. He just kept pulling.

Aliki picked up a photograph from the floor and brought it close to the candle. I noticed that there were a lot of photographs scattered around.

'Look. My brother – dead.'

His eyelids were lowered slightly. His lips pursed. As beautiful as a marble statue. If you asked me whether I thought death had ruined the harmony of his beauty, I would say no, definitely not; if anything he looked more exquisite than ever. It's the truth and I'm not afraid to say it. It's what I saw.

When they realised what had happened, they panicked. The collector kept his head, and took control of the situation. He called for Stelios and his father and told them very clearly that there had been an accident. He asked for their help, knowing that he could trust them absolutely. Father and son set to work and loosened an enormous number of floor tiles in the cellar, and started digging a hole. Then they buried the body.

It was after that, I imagine, that the vast wardrobe was pushed up against the door leading down to the basement. Perhaps it was then that Stelios and his father moved into the Aino on a permanent basis. Functioning both as caretakers and guards, two loyal dogs. But I can't be sure.

The days went by, and Aliki still hadn't heard from her brother, not even a phone call. At least she knew where to look; he'd scribbled it down for her on a piece of paper – the address of that hotel with the funny name where he was staying. He was always very careful to make sure she knew where she could find him. She had never needed to track him down before, and anyway, she knew that he would prefer it if she didn't turn up at the sort of places he went to. But this was different.

I won't let the story of how Aliki managed to find them take up much space. It was really rather simple. After spending several days watching the hotel from the outside, and never once seeing her brother either go in or come out, she decided to go inside and introduce herself. It was almost midnight, the reception desk was deserted, but there was someone sitting in the lobby. It was Ioanna Chryssovergis, making the strangest little noises, something between a sigh and a belch. This was not the only sign of her inebriation. Aliki, of course, had no idea who the woman was, but sat down next to her anyway and started asking her a lot of questions, if she had seen a handsome young man with black hair and dark eyes around the hotel. The reaction she got, as well as the answers, made her suspicious, so she persisted with her interrogation, until the drunken actress pulled out one of her favourite sayings, namely that beautiful people who die young are very lucky. Aliki realised instantly what had happened. She shot to her feet and started screaming, screaming at the top of her lungs, screaming her heart out. Nobody and nothing could stop her.

I don't know if Aliki's howls were powerful enough to jolt Chryssovergis out of her drunken stupor, but they certainly were sufficiently forceful to make the collector wake up in a state of shock and confusion and come haring down the stairs to see what was going on. In one single, quick move, he managed to secure the girl's arms behind her back and then he led, almost lifted, her upstairs. She was locked up for three days. She saw nobody, except the collector, who spent most of the period of her incarceration with her, talking to her constantly. About life, the universe, the human race, and death, but mostly about her brother.

I am in no doubt that Filippos Argyriadis is capable of exercising a great deal of charm on absolutely anyone, and I am also in no doubt that Aliki was extremely vulnerable at that time. As a result, a sort of bridge was built between the two of them, a bridge built of complicity. That's not of course the way she wanted me to see it, but this is how I see it:

In the state Aliki was in, it was quite impossible for her to cope with anything, even the most basic things. She was suddenly all alone in the world again, a drug addict with compromised judgement. For her to start a court case against a group of five such powerful and respected individuals, would have required a strength that she simply didn't possess. These people, on the other hand, as Argyriadis made abundantly clear to her, were willing to support her and to fill the vacuum created by her brother's death as best they could. He convinced her that the cause of death was nothing more than bad luck, because it was quite beyond the realms of possibility that anyone could have wanted to take his life, her brother who was born to be worshipped. She didn't find it at all hard to believe the collector when he told her how much he admired and loved Ilias. The birdcage in the garden was proof enough of that. Later on, she was introduced to the others. They were all very affectionate and solicitous. They were like a family. They cared.

There's also the fact that the sect was very open-handed and gave her a very generous weekly allowance. How else could she have continued to support her habit now that her brother was dead? I know it sounds harsh, but that was the reality she was facing.

By the time I appeared at the Aino, this relationship had been in place for five whole years.

'I never stopped coming here to talk to my brother. I firmly believe that one day we'll meet again. I picture him down there, and it doesn't scare me at all, you know. He'll always be beautiful. I know it sounds insane, but I'm sure that even his skeleton, his bones, are little works of art.'

The smell of the flowers, both the fresh and the rotten suddenly made me feel nauseous.

'The first time I saw you,' she started, and then broke off.

'You were scared,' I said, trying to help her along.

'I was.'

'You were worried that I'd share the same fate.'

'I worried that you were in danger.'

'Yes, but I don't look anything like your brother, so I think I'm pretty safe on that score. I can assure you that whatever their interest in me, it's not my irresistible beauty.'

'I know what their interest is.'

'You do?'

'Yes. I know exactly what it was that drew them to you in the first place.'

'What was?'

'*Phi Beta Kappa.*'

She registered my surprise, but went on.

'I've been reading their notes. I know a lot of things. That might be why I was able to open up to you so easily from the start. I felt that I already knew you. I read everything there was to read about you. Almost everything. There is one envelope that concerns you that I am not allowed to touch. It holds your secret. The one you confided to the group at the meeting on the roof terrace. I know everything except that.'

(I knew it; my secret would remain safely buried forever.)

'It's fascinating,' she went on, 'seeing how they operate, step by step, watching them besiege their subject, how they change direction, rather like crabs do, only to return suddenly to attack. They may go round in circles, go off at tangents, but they never lose focus, they never lose sight of what they want to research, what lies at the heart of the matter in each case.'

I asked her what the heart of the matter was in my case. She looked at me coldly, as though she had suddenly realised that she had given too much away. I reminded her that more serious matters than that already bound us together, and that whatever happened, my time at the Aino was more or less up, my programme had come to an end. She was convinced.

'It's all about the arrogance of knowledge, the absurdity of knowledge, the addictive nature of knowledge. That was it in your case, if you must know. Basically, they wanted to assess the damage that an obsession with knowledge can do to a personality in a young kid. That's what they call you, you know, in the notes, they always refer to you as "the kid". It's because you're the youngest they've ever had here, the youngest guest. Almost all of them really like and respect you. But they think that your passion for learning is over the top, is somehow unnatural, and you're in danger of neglecting other essential things in life as a result. They wondered what your reaction would be if they tempted you with some exotic piece of information, something you would find really exciting. And a lot else besides. They've thought of many things about you during this time, and written a great deal too. But that's all I'm prepared to say at the moment. Don't ask me to tell you any more.'

There was something in her voice that made it clear that she had no intention of going further. We went upstairs together, very cautiously. When we had re-emerged into Stelios's room, Aliki, taking every possible precaution, slipped in to the hallway while I jumped out of the window into the garden. I went up to my room and locked the door.

I spent the next two hours there, motionless, staring into space like the living dead. Then I changed into the smartest clothes I had with me, and when it was time I went up to the roof terrace. For my farewell dinner.

thirty

I'd like to insert a short parenthesis before I return to the story. Aliki told me about some of the previous guests at the Aino. I remember some of them: there was a talented pianist who could perform phenomenal computational feats; there was a man who had survived a plane crash, a world class chess player who had worked out the most involved philosophy based on the rules and dynamics of chess; and a middle-aged migraine sufferer who had the most amazing hallucinations during attacks, which she was able to describe in fascinating detail. I often think about these characters, think about them together, assorted flowers arranged in the same bouquet. I wonder where they are now, what their impressions of the Aino had been. There are another two faces that I see alongside theirs, the stunning escort, and the intellectually curious archaeologist. We all bear the same stamp. End of digression.

The light, the shadows cast by the trees, the colour of the sky, were exactly the same as the last time we had all gathered together up here. Even the weather vane, that old iron cockerel, was pointing his beak in exactly the same direction, only this time the entire scene was charged with an uncomfortable sense of formality. A long table had been laid with the finest china, and heavy silverware. The folding director's chairs were gone and in their place were austere looking high-back wooden dining chairs. Two waiters had been positioned discreetly to one side, ready to spring into action at the slightest signal from Argyriadis.

We took our places at table immediately and our glasses were filled with wine. A toast was made: to our happy acquaintance, which, although it had come to an end, would open new and unexpected paths for us in the future. Simos Skouris. He liked to play master of ceremonies on festive occasions. The director was seated beside me, spreading *pâté de foie gras* onto tiny little crackers with elegant knife strokes. I had never really noticed his fingers before. They were long, pink and puffy, and he was wearing a ring with a stone in the middle on one of them. They were patrician hands, clearly unaccustomed to manual work. I pictured them squeezing the life out of Ilias Alvertos, pulling relentlessly at the silk. He put his knife down on his side plate, and let his hands relax on top of the tablecloth.

'Have you been observing my hands?'

'No. I was looking at your ring.'

I had to struggle to contain my discomfort and seem natural. It was even more of a struggle to stop thinking about all the concerns that were flooding into my mind. I seemed distracted, out of humour. It took three attempts on the part of Filippos Argyriadis to ask me a question from the other side of the table before I caught it.

'Oh, yes, I have,' I eventually answered.

The question was whether I had made a note of that date, as he had instructed me to. He was satisfied with my answer.

Meanwhile, dinner was served. I had ostrich meat for the first time in my life, with black rice. I started eating, without really tasting anything.

'You see, I was right!' The photographer leant over from my left and whispered. 'I told you it would be an interesting experience!'

It may well have been interesting for them; for me it was far more than that.

'Well?' She clearly wanted confirmation.

How could this woman, with her pleasant and sensitive demeanour, have shown such an utter lack of sensitivity by taking reels and reels of photographs of Ilias Alvertos when he was not yet cold? I thought back to our trip on that abandoned ship. I knew at the time that the purpose of the outing was for her to find out exactly what I knew about Ilias Alvertos and how I had come by the information. I couldn't help wondering what would have happened to me that day if my answers had not been so reassuring.

'What a piece of bad luck that you never got to see the show properly,' announced Ioanna Chryssovergis. I hadn't seen her since that night when she had been sure that her association with me had brought her bad luck.

'Damned unlucky. Damned unlucky,' piped up Skouris.

Simos Skouris had not been part of the sect at the time of Alvertos's death. He had never seen him. At least, not alive. However, he still had an opinion about everything. He had heard them talk about it, he'd read all the notes, he'd seen the photographs. Surely. How else could he possibly have become a member, the fifth link? You would think that Chryssovergis's sudden decision to get married (and if my calculations are right, it wasn't long after the so-called accident) had a lot to do with the episode. It was a kind of cover for the benefit of the outside world, an approximation of a normal life.

'I do hope that our bond will endure into the future. Don't you?'

'You can be sure of it.' The collector answered Skouris's

question in my stead. 'There are so many ties that bind us, indissoluble ties.'

I imagined myself getting to my feet in the middle of the meal and in a calm, steady voice announcing that I knew everything about the fate that had befallen their handsome guest. Everything. What happened to him and where he was now. Then it occurred to me that it was just about the most idiotic thing I could do in the circumstances. I had to wait for these last few hours to pass, get away safely from the hotel, and then make some decisions.

'I'll take your advice after all,' said Halkiolakis, squeezing my knee at the same time. He was talking about alternative endings for his script. My knee went numb and it was a while before the circulation returned to it.

When it did, another feeling started to return too. Fury. Everything was so simple and so easy. So convenient. They could end another human life, just like that, and then get on with their lives again as though nothing had happened. The body disappears, the relatives say nothing, nobody's interested. Subsequent guests arrive and get added to the list of guinea pigs, and Alvertos is nothing more than one more name on the files, another portrait hanging in the Aino collection. What, I wondered, would happen if I decided to put the cat among the pigeons? What would happen if I went to the police with what I knew?

'Before I forget! When you get back to your room, you'll see an envelope on your bed,' said Paraschis quietly. 'It's the balance of what's due to you.'

I'd completely forgotten that they still owed me money. Of course the photographer was no mind reader but the way she said it, at that precise moment, struck me as an attempt to buy my silence.

What would happen – I asked myself again – if I decided to go to the station and tell them everything I knew about the goings on in that basement all those years ago? One thing was for sure – I would have to wave goodbye to Aino. Argyriadis would never hand over the codex if I did that. He was so right when he said that there were a number of ties that bound us now. It had only taken a fortnight for me to get trapped in their tantalising web, only two weeks for them to become important to me.

How could I forget that these were the only people that I had ever confided my big secret in? That was all it took for a sense of loyalty to spring up in me. But I want to be perfectly clear about one thing: if they did decide to break my confidence, I wouldn't get into any serious trouble as a result. It wouldn't get me into any kind of legal mess, it wouldn't ruin my reputation, one way or another. It couldn't do me much immediate harm, and was not something they could use to blackmail me with in the future either. Still, it was very personal; I had laid bare my soul, and even today, I have never had the courage to repeat the confession. And that meant something. It meant something then and it means something now.

'It's only natural that we should all be a little sad today,' said the collector.

He'd been looking at me for some time with those penetrating eyes, almost certainly trying to read my thoughts. I looked back at him. It was a breathless moment, a void. My stomach tensed up in the same way it would if I was about to vomit. He raised his glass.

'May Aino always afford us her protection!'

Aino! Aino! I had held the manuscript in my hands. I had turned its pages. I had touched it. I had seen it. It existed. It was real. It was real.

But was it? Was it real? Was it?

Feelings of doubt suddenly cut off my circulation; I had to face the possibility that they were toying with me. What if the entire story about Aino was an elaborate fabrication, a joke? My education, my experience, did not stretch to telling a genuine Byzantine manuscript from a fake. My throat went dry, paralysed, making any attempt at swallowing food out of the question.

'They wanted to see what the effect of offering you some tantalizing piece of information would be on your behaviour, how you'd react.' Aliki's words.

Was it so completely implausible, though, that they could have commissioned someone to make them the codex? After all, we were talking about the same people who had managed to acquire a caged hawk in a matter of hours just to amuse Ilias Alvertos. If they really put their mind to something, I was sure there was very little they couldn't do. It wouldn't have taken much to nail a faded-looking sign with the name Aino painted on it outside the building, and they were all set. The great deception could begin. At first they were testing my curiosity, then my pride, before moving on to my enthusiasm. A puppet, moving to the rhythms dictated by their clever, nimble fingers.

And who could blame them? Paraschis had been very straightforward with me right from the start: the purpose of my stay was to enable them to study me. I was paid to make myself available, so I had no right to feel either duped, or that I had grounds for complaint. They had the right to devise whatever tricks best suited their purposes.

I remembered that day when I tried to worm the information about Aino out of the supposedly naïve Simos Skouris. Right! Which of us was the naïve one? Bet I really gave them something to laugh about that day! That will have gone down in the annals, as well as everything else, every embarrassing moment, every time I lost my temper, not to mention their unspoken disappointment with me. The idea of it!

Suddenly, in the depths of my despair, just as the waiters were serving the wonderful desserts, small mounds of cream swathed in colourful syrups in peacock feather formation, something else occurred to me, something which shed a shard of sharp light on the situation.

Although everything suggested that I had been played for a fool, there still seemed compelling reasons why the Aino story should be genuine. Not genuine simply in terms of the source of the myth, but, what was infinitely more extraordinary, genuine in terms of the very concrete threat the goddess posed. Everything that had happened so far pointed to this conclusion. How? It's perfectly simple: the day that Filippos Argyriadis revealed the codex to me ('It is necessary to feel it between your fingers, to touch it for yourself, the thing itself' he'd said to me on that occasion), the very same day (well, technically the same day because our meeting took place after midnight), their most closely guarded secret came to light – that of the disappearance of Ilias Alvertos. Didn't that prove that the omniscient Aino was very real and was punishing him for betraying her?

The stress of the last few hours built up in my stomach, assuming the form of a heavy stone. A large, heavy stone, which was growing all the time and putting more and more pressure on my stomach until it became quite unbearable. I stood up, left the table and staggered out to the western corner of the roof terrace. Bent over double, for the first time in God knows how many years, I vomited.

thirty-one

The envelope with the money was lying on my bed, just as Paraschis had promised. I tossed it to the bottom of my suitcase and started packing. My books, my good luck teddy bear, my tape player. I wasn't due to leave until the following morning, but had decided not to wait. Absolutely certain no one was around, I went downstairs and slipped out into the darkness of the streets outside. I walked around in the dead of the damp night for hours, not really knowing where I was going or what I wanted to do. If I hadn't been dragging a suitcase around with me, I could have gone on walking till morning. I was attracting the oddest stares from the creatures of the night as I crossed their territory with my battered old suitcase. I could hear them whispering as I went by, inviting me to join their world, but I didn't stop, just kept on walking straight ahead, giving the misleading impression that I had somewhere to go. The truth is that I did, not somewhere to go in the ordinary sense, but somewhere to get away from, to leave the Aino as far behind me as possible, and I was content to allow my footsteps to lead me.

'Fancy some of this? Some of this, then?' Attempts to tempt me.

I had to get away without looking back. I wanted to

wake up the next morning and not remember a thing. I wanted not to have taken Paraschis up on her offer in the first place.

Eventually I took a taxi home. I unlocked the door, turned the lights on, saw my things: my bed, the fridge, my records. Everything was just as I'd left it, yet nothing was the same. Things change along with their owner, and this owner had come back a very different man.

thirty-two

This is the thirty-second time I'm writing in this notebook. It's been almost four months since I first put pen to paper. The narrative is drawing to a close, and I have succeeded in my original aim: small, shadowy details, in imminent danger of being swallowed up irretrievably in the darkness have been preserved; jumbled memories have been restored to the correct time frame. But that's not all. Something else has happened, something unexpected. Whenever I started on a description of something, knowing in advance what I wanted to say, various shades, tones and scents would resurface through God only knows what unseen cracks in my memory into my consciousness at precisely that moment, after lying quiescent for so many years. I would welcome them with startled delight, restoring them all to their proper place. This makes me believe that in future there might be similar unexpected visits from dormant memories. I think it would be easy enough for me to sort them out and arrange them within the body of the story; after all I have retraced my steps on countless occasions before in order to add in forgotten detail.

In the past, I used to wonder whether my recollection of the entire episode was nothing more than complete fabrication, the product of a sick cell nestling somewhere in my brain, persuading me that I had actually lived through these things and met all those people. A projection. The madman can convince himself that he has experienced a real situation, and can even reconstruct it with disarming accuracy. But I actually saw the Aino a short while ago with my own eyes; the fact that it's now called 'Alabaster' is of little consequence. I saw Aliki, and spoke to her; I spoke to Stelios too, so I needn't torture myself with this insane notion again. And I'll never question my own sanity. Never again, and I'll try to stop tracing the workings of my mind in such detail. It's not good for me.

When I left the Aino and went back to my old life, I was under a lot of pressure and had a great deal of reading to catch up on. Exams were just round the corner, and I hadn't opened a book for an entire fortnight. I was determined not only to graduate that year but to do so with first class honours. It was a race against time. My pride would not have settled for anything less, as the collector would no doubt have commented. Being so busy turned out to be a blessing, even though it did not keep me completely immune to flashbacks of my days at the Aino. The faces, snippets of conversation, entire scenes, thoughts and speculations, got their share of my attention.

Everything came off the way I'd planned: I did extremely well and managed to enrol at an Italian university for post-graduate work that autumn. I tidied up my affairs, settled all my bills and found myself at a loose end for three whole months. Three months of freedom, and with money in my pocket too, for a change – thanks to the sect. The first adjustment I made was to my sleeping patterns. I started spending much longer in bed, only rising in the late afternoon to go down to the gaming arcade, which was going strong at the time. I'd stay there until late evening, overloading my senses with flashing space ships and revolving fruit. It was the best way to keep my mind off things. It kept me sane, even though I could see that the balance was very fine. Summer: heat and electronic games. One day I finally cracked up. I saw Ilias Alvertos in my sleep. Dressed in a red cassock he came limping across to me, and although it was undoubtedly the same man, his face looked very different from the one in his sister's photographs. 'You must help me,' he said, moving closer and pointing to his bare foot. He sat down on the floor and turned his heel inwards so that I could see the sole of his foot. There was a sharp black thorn rammed into the flesh. 'Help me pull it out,' he said, forcing me without the slightest physical coercion to bend over and take a look. I lowered my face down to the level of his foot in an attempt to see where the edge of the thorn was so I could extract it. 'You've got to help,' he repeated.

That was the dream. Alvertos's cry for help was so desperate and so urgent that it really shook me up.

I started to re-evaluate everything: the sect, Aliki, Alvertos, Aino. It was torture, and my sleep was tortured, plagued with nightmares. It got to the stage where I was getting as little as four or five hours a night, sometimes fewer. My nerves were in shreds and I would fly off the handle at the most ridiculous things, like my neighbour sneezing, for instance. I became very jumpy and everyday noises, car horns and the like, would make me leap out of my skin. The heat had really got to me and I had no appetite for food whatsoever. It was an overwhelming sense of responsibility which made sleep so elusive. Perhaps the dream had affected me more than I realised. I heard a voice telling me that I was the only person in the universe who could expose the injustice of Ilias Alvertos's death, that it was incumbent on me to pull back all those perfumed veils concealing his rotten flesh – in other words, that I should do what I had already contemplated doing. Report the murder.

I tried to rationalise this, and think through all the possible consequences such an action would have, beyond giving me the satisfaction of knowing that I had done the right thing – whatever that means.

Apart from anything else, how could I possibly know what Ilias Alvertos would have wanted? Assuming the body turns into the soul after death, and that the soul continues to take an interest in the affairs of the living, how could I possibly know whether or not Ilias Alvertos's soul would have wanted me to go sticking my nose into this? After all it would certainly cause significant disruption to his sister's life. Because I had to weigh up that aspect of the business too – how it would affect Aliki if she lost yet another family, however bogus it was.

The hardest issue for me was not Aliki but whether I would be able to confront the five members of the sect. Would I really be able to bring myself to betray the friendship and the respect they had shown me so generously? Would I be able to betray my own feelings for them? Would I really be able to risk access to the Aino codex and sacrifice such a rare opportunity? I had often fantasised about publishing articles in renowned archaeological journals, making my name in the process and paving the way for a distinguished academic career. Now look at me – through an impossible series of impossible coincidences a dream subject, a lost goddess, has landed on my plate. But if I wasn't careful, I would lose her, and the bright future she could bring me, just as suddenly as I'd found her.

In the end it was that prospect, that by doing nothing I would secure a bright future for myself, that made me choose the opposite course and do the noble, the right thing. Feels a bit foolish now. On the 14th August, a Wednesday, with the thermometer nudging forty, I went down to the police station and made an official statement.

Then I locked myself in my flat after stocking up on sleeping pills to help me shut down for as long as possible. There was no other way of getting through the next ten days. Phone off the hook. Shutters closed. I drank huge amounts of water, ate practically nothing. Emptied out my brain. No guilt, no concerns, no suspense, no sense of satisfaction either. But not indifferent either. Just blank. Empty.

My self-imposed incarceration lasted ten days after which I started going out again. But my movements were all mechanical. I attended to all the practical matters, talked to people, read the newspaper, got on buses, doing everything without any deeper sense of what was going on in the world around me. I realised that something had died inside me, that I had gone completely numb. Like that feeling you get after the dentist has been busy with you, and you try to pull at your anaesthetized cheek – that pretty much describes my entire being. At first I was worried that this might be the symptom of a more serious disorder, but even this fear did not manage to reawaken my old ability to feel – the fear was flabby, it was superficial. Everything was so shallow. I hadn't the slightest desire for anything, not for tastes, not for images, not for bodies. So shallow.

I didn't want to hear about it; I didn't want to know what happened as a result of my visit to the station. I buried my head deep in the sand, knowing full well that the relevant mechanisms, working to their own rules and regulations, would be in motion. It was out of my hands.

One evening as I was approaching my building, I noticed a man about thirty metres away from me on the opposite corner, standing there in the darkness, half-leaning on a car bonnet. I recognised him the second he looked up. Petros Halkiolakis. Despite the numbness engulfing my heart, I instinctively quickened my pace and walked in his direction.

Then I heard an unfamiliar voice behind me whisper my name. This was followed by a tap on the shoulder. I turned and saw a face I'd never seen before.

He was about forty, foreign, possibly Mexican. He was holding a piece of paper full of scribbles in a foreign language. He started reading from it, his voice struggling to produce the right Greek sounds. Somehow I managed to distil the gist of what he was saying:

'The best thing you can do is disappear. The man who is reading this to you is prepared to bury a sharp knife into your soft belly. As soon as he finishes reading this, he will turn round and look at me. If I give him the signal, if I nod, he'll do it. That's for me to decide and I'll wait till the last minute before I make up my mind. If he just turns and walks away, run. You haven't got time to lose.'

It was obvious that he hadn't the faintest idea what he was reading to me. When he finished he turned to look at the director, who screwed up his eyes and walked away quickly. By the time I turned round to start running, the street was empty.

Unbelievable! That shock was exactly what I needed – the slap that brings you round after fainting. I came to my senses. Halkiolakis had accomplished what he set out to do: scare the life out of me. I knew how vengeful he could be. I remembered what Paraschis had told me about how he had settled accounts with Argyriadis *père*. My first reaction was to report the incident to the police, but then I reconsidered, deciding instead to follow the advice communicated to me in such an original way, and left for Italy immediately.

I found out about the progress of the case from a friend, a student in the law department, who had the opportunity to follow the entire case up close. He told me everything in elaborate detail, and was careful to send me everything the papers were writing about it.

The first thing I need to get straight is that nobody in the sect ever tried to deny the charge. The police got a warrant to search the basement and everyone cooperated fully. An autopsy was carried out. There was no point in anything anymore. Everything had been judged. Filippos Argyriadis shouldered the blame. The leader 'confessed' that it was he who had tightened the silken noose around the neck of their guest, and that he bore sole responsibility for his death. Halkiolakis agreed. The others kept quiet. They followed an agreed line, they were word perfect and not one contradiction appeared in their testimonies. They all went along with the lie that their leader had chosen to tell, and never once challenged him. Those 'second sides' I talked about on the very first page of this account had come into play at the most crucial moment.

The court ruled malice aforethought and handed down what was in the minds of many a stiff sentence: fifteen years' imprisonment.

I went to pieces. I wished I could undo what I had done. But it was one of those irreversible things.

The sect disbanded. All because of me. Tina Paraschis went abroad. Petros Halkiolakis moved back to the island where he'd grown up, Ioanna Chryssovergis gave fewer and fewer performances. (Perhaps the fact that Simos Skouris shortly thereafter developed serious health problems also had something to do with that.) The Aino turned to Alabaster. Aliki, however, experienced a rebirth. I have no idea how the miracle occurred, but it did. Her total breakdown might have forced her to make radical decisions about her life.

Filippos Argyriadis is due to be released in four or five years, after his sentence was reduced for good behaviour. At least that's what I assumed from what Stelios told me that night at the Alabaster.

I don't think there's anything left for me to say. That's the end of the story. But its heroes are all still alive, and as long as its heroes are alive, a story is rarely over.

ROME — 22ND DECEMBER 2003

At last! I'd been looking for this notebook everywhere. I spent eleven whole days looking for it. I'd just about given up.

It's been four years since I last wrote anything. Meanwhile, I've moved house a total of five times, each time making absolutely sure that there was no chance of the notebook going astray. It always went in my green leather briefcase along with all my important documents. Nobody ever touches that except me, and I would wait until my bookcase had been properly organised before I took it out again and hid it behind those weighty tomes of Byzantine history, pinioned against the wooden back panel, where it would lie undisturbed until it was time to move on again.

At least that's what I thought, because eleven days ago I needed it so I could write about the latest unexpected development in the saga, and when I pulled back those heavy, dusty volumes I saw that it was missing. I felt my scalp go numb with shock, and I wouldn't be surprised if the hairs on my head had bristled like a cat's. I had no idea where to look. When something has a permanent place and never moves from that place, the possibilities of it being mislaid or misfiled are limited. Your brain stops working, and you feel that you'd be wasting your time looking for it. I immediately thought of L. I am grown up, and no longer go looking for metaphysical explanations. I prefer the rational route. Somebody had obviously moved it from its hiding place. The only person who has the opportunity to do so was L, nobody else. The only problem was that L and I hadn't spoken to each other for months, so if she had the notebook, I would never see it again, as I hadn't the faintest idea where she was, nor did I have any means of tracking her down. I didn't despair though, and started to search for it in the most likely and unlikely places. A few minutes ago I unearthed it from beneath the rug in the bedroom. It was pure coincidence, a stroke of luck, unless it was my unconscious that led me there, as it had once done to a drawer in a hotel wardrobe. It occurred to me that the slight bump I felt on the naked sole of my foot every time I got out of bed at night to go to the bathroom might just be what I was looking for.

It proved what I had always believed, that there is no such thing as a safe hiding place, because in time even the most carefully hidden things creep to the surface. It was just as well that I hadn't written down absolutely everything in the notebook and had kept some details to myself, Anyway, the orange notebook turned up, was safely back in my possession, and that's all that matters. Now I can get on with what it was I wanted to write.

Eleven days ago, I received a letter by registered mail. It was in a small envelope, and contained a handwritten letter in violet ink, a small, regular script. Filippos Argyriadis's hand. It probably makes more sense for me to reproduce it verbatim than to summarise the contents:

It took me five months to track you down and find out your full postal address. I understand that you move house regularly. That's good; I by contrast am a creature of permanence, not to say absolute immobility, judging by recent standards. In my efforts to find you, I have been assisted by a distant relative, a nephew of sorts, a student, who attended some of your lectures in the past. It's a very small world indeed. Don't be surprised if some of your colleagues, or some former neighbours, start telling you about some inquisitive young man asking them a lot of questions. They might even describe him to you: tall, thin, bespectacled and his ears stick out. Well, that's my nephew. He was one of your most enthusiastic students. You may even remember him, but I'd rather not mention his name. You have a description. That should suffice.

I want you to know that I have been following your career and am aware of the recognition you have won in your field. When I tell you how pleased I am for you, I do so in all sincerity. I had every confidence that you would distinguish yourself. I remember you so vividly...You had a remarkable mind for one so young, and infallible judgement. Almost infallible, that is. I try to picture you as you are today, mature, still young of course, but mature. You must be around thirty-five, according to my calculations. Those last childlike traces will have disappeared behind that grave and unsmiling facade of yours. My nephew once described you to me, and I think it's a pity that you allowed yourself to run to fat; a lean physique is so much better suited to a quick and restless mind such as yours. But I also hear that you are less unsmiling these days. That is a real gain, believe me.

As for me, the most important thing is that I am a free man. The age of darkness has come to an end. I'm back in the light. Free and also liberated from everything that burdened me in the past, the secrets. I have no more secrets. Some things were exposed, other things not, but it is a matter of indifference to me if they are exposed at some point, so it amounts to the same thing. I am empty. I am void and enjoying the feeling. It's as though I have died and am observing everything from on high. This is a very happy time for me. Your time at the Aino, meeting you, were crucial events in my life. In case you were concerned that I would harbour resentment towards you, or think ill of you, let me reassure you that neither is true. I recognise that you are not directly responsible for the part you played. I set everything in motion myself. I had a showdown with the goddess and had to take the consequences. You were simply a tool, performing a predetermined function. Deep down, I knew in advance how things were going to turn out as soon as I revealed the secret to you. The day I placed the codex in your hand, to look at, to touch, to read through, I was in no doubt at all. Aino is harsh by name and by nature.

My only concern was that you should not come to any harm. You were so young, so full of enthusiasm, and it would have been unforgivable of me to place a weapon you did not know how to use in your hands. You see, I didn't have the excuse of youth. I felt responsible for you. I told you that at the time, if you remember.

Things are very different now, of course. You are much older for a start, and secondly, you know from experience what it means to play with fire. I now want to make good on the promise I once made you. I want you to accept my father's codex, with the hope that you will treat it wisely. The burden of choice rests exclusively on your shoulders. Whatever you decide to do, you will meet no opposition from me, even in the event that you tear the parchment into a thousand tiny pieces or commit it to flames.

I imagine that you have already removed the tiny key wrapped in fabric from the envelope along with the slip of paper containing all the information you need to open the safe deposit box. Go on. Aino is in your hands now.

In closing, let me make this conclusion: The revenge of the goddess, however cruel it may be, is redemptive at the same time.

My warmest wishes for the coming Christmas season and for the New Year, which is already peeping out at us from behind the curtain.

Yours etc.'

There was a rather lengthy postscript at the bottom of the page, telling me all about the sect, how it had disbanded and its members scattered. My stay at the Aino had, in this case too, been fateful. But he was quick to reassure me that

I should not feel guilty, that at the most decisive moment he had realised one thing: that his ties to those people had weakened some time before, that the way they saw things was radically different from his own perspective, and although there was a residual emotional attachment, he was glad to have broken through the blockade and escaped, freed himself. 'I just wasn't cut out for a *Phi Beta Kappa* set up,' he wrote.

That was the last thing I expected him to say. His 'second side', the side trained to coexist and coordinate with the others had, it seemed, expired.

The very next morning (without telling anybody) I left. I set off on a lightning journey and was back in a matter of only hours. I am sitting here, looking down at the codex resting on my desk. Whenever I leave the house, I secrete it behind my tall art books, and take it down as soon as I return to study it. I have read it countless times. I realise that I have unconsciously learnt entire sections of it off by heart.

There is no doubt in my mind that the codex is genuine. It's a manuscript of outstanding value, even though it has no aesthetic merit. It was crudely put together; the wooden boards that hold it are clad in inferior fabric, and it is totally devoid of decoration. No trace of miniatures, no capitals decorated in carmine. The only thing that is of any artistic interest is the final pen stroke at the end of the manuscript containing the code name of the scribe. The parchment itself is of poor quality, full of imperfections, stains and bristle roots which had not been removed from the hide with due care.

None of this matters. The power is intact. At night I turn out the lights and look at the parchment pages as they lie there, shining through the darkness in an almost phosphorescent shimmer.

I still don't know what I'm going to do with it. There are so many things I have to think through. I'm taking my time.

I look at my orange notebook and count the remaining blank pages. Just five. That'll be plenty when the time comes for me to write about the choice I eventually make. When I make it. There's no hurry, no pressure. I am at peace.

Also by Vangelis Hatziyannidis and published by Marion Boyars:

four waLLs

Translated from the Greek by Anne-Marie Stanton-Ife

'The moment he closed his lips round the laden spoon, the honey exploded inside his mouth; he felt like he was under attack from some overwhelming force... It did not take long for the aroma from the opened jar to pervade the entire room... Its presence was so manifest that Rodakis thought that it was actually visible, that it was the mist cloud enshrouding him...'

Following the death of his beekeeper father, Rodakis lives a solitary life in the old family house on a Greek island. When the village elders ask him to take in a young fugitive woman and her daughter, he reluctantly agrees, and she soon persuades him to return to the family business of making honey. Thanks to his father's secret recipe, they produce a delicious honey that becomes highly sought after, and the woman's daughter, Rosa, comes to depend on Rodakis when her mother meets with a fatal accident. But everyone wants to get their hands on the secret honey recipe, and Rodakis is captured and imprisoned by a jealous monk who wants the power of the honey for himself.

Alone on the island, Rosa goes in search of her real father but it becomes clear that she is ignorant of the acceptable boundaries of sexual relationships and he decides she must be kept locked in her room. There is only one thing to do. Rodakis must use his precious secret recipe to bargain for Rosa's release.

'Vangelis Hatziyannidis' first novel delightfully blends the serious...themes of imprisonment and solitude with humour, humility, horribly violent deaths, coincidences and miracles – all of which add up to a witty fable, satisfyingly replete with the essential ingredients of magical realism.' *The Guardian*

£7.99/$14.95

ISBN: 0-7145-3122-7 ~ 13 digit ISBN: 978-0-7145-3122-9